"Give me one reason why I would even consider marrying you—"

"Well, most women start with my wallet," he drawled softly, and she gave an incredulous laugh. In her opinion, all the money in the world wouldn't compensate for being in a loveless marriage.

"I'm not interested in your money. Money doesn't make a family happy," she said. "It's love and attention from parents that does that."

"I agree," he said confidently, his dark eyes fixed on her face. "And Rosa will have that. You cannot possibly be pretending that she won't benefit from also living with her father."

She could barely hide her frustration. "But we don't love each other."

He frowned impatiently. "I admire you professionally and I appreciate your deep love for Rosa. Mutual understanding is all we need. I don't need you to love me."

She looked at him helplessly. "And if I say no?"

SARAH MORGAN trained as a nurse and has since worked in a variety of health-related jobs. Married to a gorgeous businessman who still makes her knees knock, she spends most of her time trying to keep up with their two little boys, but manages to sneak off occasionally to indulge her passion for writing romance. Sarah loves outdoor life and is an enthusiastic skier and walker. Whatever she is doing, her head is always full of new characters, and she is addicted to happy endings.

THE ITALIAN DOCTOR'S WIFE

SARAH MORGAN

MEDITERRANEAN DOCTORS

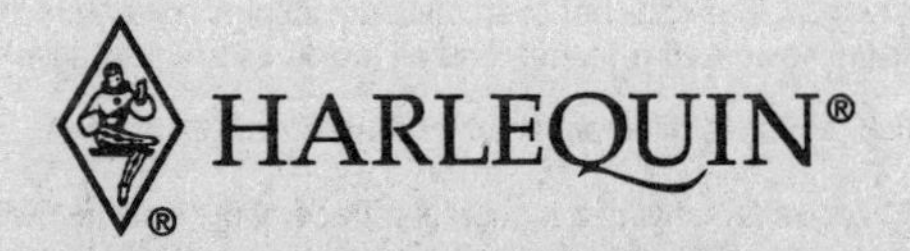

TORONTO • NEW YORK • LONDON
AMSTERDAM • PARIS • SYDNEY • HAMBURG
STOCKHOLM • ATHENS • TOKYO • MILAN • MADRID
PRAGUE • WARSAW • BUDAPEST • AUCKLAND

ISBN 0-373-82007-0

THE ITALIAN DOCTOR'S WIFE

First North American Publication 2004.

This edition published by arrangement with Harlequin Books S.A.

www.eHarlequin.com

Printed in U.S.A.

PROLOGUE

DOMENICO SANTINI slammed open the door of the exclusive clinic, his sensual mouth set in a grim line. Every muscle in his body was tense, every nerve ending responding to the anger that simmered inside his powerful frame.

He strode across the elegant reception area towards his brother's consulting room, totally oblivious to the rapt female attention which followed his progress.

Under strict instructions to allow no one to see the boss without an appointment, the receptionist half rose to her feet and then sat down again, her knees weak as she recognised the visitor. Even the threat of losing her job wouldn't have given her the courage to try and stop Domenico Santini.

And he knew it.

The self-assured stride, the arrogant tilt of that dark head and the bored, slightly disdainful look on his sinfully handsome face were the mark of a man who knew that his authority wouldn't be challenged.

He moved through the foyer with the lethal grace of a jungle cat, and the receptionist stared, feasting her eyes on the luxuriant black hair, the smouldering dark eyes and the muscular, athletic body.

The newspapers and gossip magazines didn't do the man justice.

He was staggeringly good-looking.

Ferociously intelligent, monumentally rich and wickedly handsome, Domenico Santini was every woman's fantasy.

'Don't even think about it,' her fellow receptionist drawled softly, following the direction of her gaze. 'He's way out of your league.'

'He's stunning.'

'He's also dangerous,' her friend muttered. 'He's a very famous heart surgeon, did you know that? Children's heart surgeon. What a joke! The man must have broken as many hearts as he's mended in his time. He only has to snap those clever fingers and women leap into his bed. Lucky them.'

It was a woman who was on Nico's mind as he opened the door of his brother's consulting room, pausing only long enough to check that he wasn't with a patient.

'I need to talk to you—' His tone was curt and he spoke in Italian as the brothers always did when they were alone together.

Carlo Santini leaned back in his chair, his dark eyes watchful. 'So—talk.'

Two years younger than Nico and generally considered to be the more approachable of the two brothers, he waved a hand towards a chair, but Nico ignored the gesture and instead opened his briefcase and retrieved a slim file which he tossed onto his brother's desk.

'Read that.'

Carlo stared at him for a long moment and then lowered his eyes to the file, opening it slowly and perusing the contents.

While he read, Nico paced across the room, his broad shoulders tense as he stared out of the window across the expensively manicured grounds of his brother's clinic. Occasionally he glanced over his shoulder, his expression impatient as he waited for his brother to finish digesting the contents of the file.

'So?' Finally Carlo lowered the file. 'This girl had donor insemination in my clinic.' His tone was noticeably cool. 'I don't know why you have a file on her, but if you've come to me for more information then you're going to be disappointed. You're my brother and I love you, but I won't discuss my patients with you.'

'This isn't a clinic matter, it's a family matter.' Nico's black brows met in a frown. He'd expected Carlo to react to the name in the file but he'd forgotten just how many women trooped through his brother's world-famous infertility clinic every year. 'And I'm not asking you to break patient confidentiality. Look at the name again.'

'Harrington. Abby Harrington—it doesn't ring any bells.' Carlo peered more closely at the photo. 'I've definitely never seen her before. She's gorgeous. There's no way I would have forgotten a face and a body like that.'

'Then let me jog your memory,' Nico's expression darkened. 'She was Lucia's friend at school. Remember the shy little mouse who we thought might have a stabilising influence on our dizzy sister?'

Carlo's eyes narrowed. 'Vaguely. What about her?'

'And do you remember what happened two years ago?' Nico's tone was lethally soft. 'Lucia came to me with a sob story about a friend who couldn't have children.'

Carlo frowned. 'Yes, I remember that. The woman was in her late thirties and her husband was infertile and—' He broke off and his eyes travelled from his brother's icy expression to the photo in the file. 'Are you suggesting what I think you're suggesting? This is *never* the same girl.'

'It's the same girl,' Nico growled softly. 'As you can see, Lucia's *friend* wasn't in her late thirties or happily married.'

Carlo winced. 'I'm beginning to understand your interest. If my memory serves me correctly, that was the one and only occasion that we've managed to persuade you to be a donor for my clinic.'

Nico's jaw tightened. 'Fathering children indiscriminately with no say in their upbringing has never appealed to me, as you well know.'

Carlo held his gaze. 'But you agreed to do it for Lucia's friend.'

Nico dragged long fingers through his luxuriant black

hair and gave a growl of anger and frustration. '*Dio*, I was totally taken in by her sob story—how her friend's husband couldn't father children and how devastated they were....'

Carlo stared at the file. 'And you really think that this is the same woman?'

Nico's mouth tightened. 'I know it is.'

Carlo let out a long breath. 'Well, if you're right, it certainly seems as though our little sister might have been economical with the truth,' he observed, his eyes fixed on the photograph in the file. 'She looks nearer twenty than forty.'

'She's twenty-four,' Nico ground out, 'but she was twenty-two when she came to your clinic—*twenty-two*.' His voice was raw as he emphasised the words. 'And she has never been married.'

'I didn't see her, Nico.' Carlo put the file down, his expression serious. 'Come to think of it, I think I *was* due to see her but then there was a family crisis and she had to see one of my colleagues instead.'

'That was cleverly arranged,' Nico said bitterly. 'Who do you think engineered the family crisis that kept you away from the clinic that day?'

Carlo pulled a face. 'Lucia?'

'If Abby Harrington had seen you personally, you might have refused to go ahead—at least with me as the donor.'

Carlo nodded. 'Because I would have known that you wouldn't agree to be a donor for a single girl.'

'But the doctor who eventually saw her didn't know that,' Nico concluded, his mouth set in a grim line. 'I suspect that Lucia had him wound round her little finger as she did the rest of us.'

Carlo shook his head in disbelief. 'She certainly thought it through.'

'If our little sister applied the same degree of thought and deviousness to a useful career then she might stop wasting her life,' Nico observed acidly. 'We all know what

Lucia is like when she wants something. She is manipulative and persuasive and she can be very, very difficult to resist. *Dio*, even knowing her as I do, I agreed to be the donor in her little scheme.'

Carlo fingered the file, his handsome face troubled. 'So how did you get this information? You know we have strict rules about confidentiality at the clinic. How can you be sure that this is your baby?'

Nico tensed and a hint of colour touched his incredible cheekbones. 'You know how strongly I feel about family. I wanted to check on the baby I fathered.' A muscle moved in his jaw. 'I knew you wouldn't give me the information I needed so I hired a private detective.'

Carlo frowned. 'But you didn't even have the girl's name. He wouldn't have been able to—'

'He's the best,' Nico interrupted smoothly. 'He found her. That's all you need to know.'

'And have you spoken to Lucia?'

'Not yet.' Nico's expression was grim. 'I'm going to see Abby Harrington first. Then I'll deal with Lucia.'

Carlo let out a long breath. 'Well, don't be *too* hard on our little sister. You're pretty strict with her, Nico.'

'If I detected the slightest evidence of common sense, I'd cease to be strict,' Nico said wearily, and Carlo nodded.

'I know—she's a total airhead and if it weren't for you she'd have come off the rails years ago because our father's too busy to notice her.' He closed the file and handed it back to his brother. 'I can't imagine how she thought she'd get away with it but I suppose there was a chance that you wouldn't find out the truth about Abby Harrington.'

'Evidently.' Nico's voice was clipped. 'Both of them must have assumed that I'd never follow it up.'

Carlo sat back in his chair, his dark eyes reflecting his concern. 'So now what?'

There was a tense silence and when Nico finally spoke his voice was hoarse. 'I want that baby.'

There was a deathly silence and for endless seconds Carlo didn't move.

Finally he spoke, his voice urgent. 'You can't do that, Nico.'

'It's my child.'

'I know that.' Carlo's eyes were fixed on his brother's face. 'And I also know what that knowledge must be doing to you in the light of what's happened to you since that baby was conceived. Nico, you've never really talked about it, but you know that if you want to—'

'I don't.' Nico's tone held a cold finality. 'I just want to talk about this girl.'

'We both know that it is one and the same subject.' Carlo said carefully. 'I know how strongly you feel about family but we both know that there's more to this than—'

'That's enough!' Nico's eyes were hard as he stared at his brother. 'This isn't about me. It's about *her*. And the child. *My* child. I feel a responsibility towards that baby, which is why I decided to check on how the family was getting on.'

'I can imagine how you must be feeling, but you agreed to be the father,' Carlo reminded him, and Nico lifted a hand to cut him off, his expression menacing.

'For a happily married couple. Not for a young, single girl with no financial or emotional support. I never would have agreed to father a child for a penniless schoolgirl!'

'She was twenty-two.'

Nico let out his breath in an impatient hiss. 'As far as her suitability for motherhood goes, she is a baby!'

Carlo looked at him through narrowed eyes. 'You've never met her. She might be a great mother.'

'I know everything I need to know about her,' Nico said flatly, 'and the more I know, the more determined I am to take the child away from her. She isn't a fit mother.'

'Calm down.' Carlo leaned back in his chair. 'That's a pretty serious accusation. What's the woman done?'

Nico gritted his teeth. 'Apart from conspiring with Lucia to lie to me so that I'd agree to father the baby? Well, for a start she puts the child in a crèche while she works as a nurse. If she wanted a child so badly, why is she working?'

'Nico, this is the twenty-first century,' Carlo pointed out quietly, his tone reasonable. 'Women work. Even women with children. And working mothers need child care.'

'She shouldn't have chosen to become a single mother if she didn't have the means to support the child,' Nico growled, and Carlo's eyes narrowed.

'Well, not everybody has unlimited funds. Maybe she had good reasons for wanting a child—'

Nico made an impatient sound. 'Why are you defending her? What possible reasons could justify a twenty-two-year-old wanting a baby? She has plenty of reproductive years ahead of her in which to marry a man and produce babies naturally.'

Carlo looked him straight in the eye. 'I'm defending her because I know that this isn't about her and the baby. Not really. It's about you,' he said softly. 'You are making this personal.'

'*Dio*, of course I'm making it personal!' Nico flashed him an impatient look. 'How do you think I feel, knowing—?'

He broke off and Carlo rose to his feet, watching his brother closely.

'You can't take her child, Nico.'

'Watch me.' Nico's expression was grim. 'And you're forgetting that it isn't just her child, it's *my* child. And according to my sources, the girl is in big trouble. She earns next to nothing as a nurse and she obviously doesn't manage her money well. At the moment she has been given two weeks' notice to find somewhere else to live because she can't keep up the rental payments. My sources tell me that she doesn't have enough money for anywhere else.

Soon my child will be homeless. Do you expect me to sit and watch while that happens?'

Carlo let out a long breath. 'I can see that the situation is less than ideal, but—'

'My child does not deserve a nomadic existence with a mother who clearly can't manage her finances well enough to keep a roof over her head,' Nico growled, and Carlo watched him thoughtfully.

'She might not be willing to give the baby up,' he pointed out, and Nico frowned dismissively.

'The girl is clearly struggling to bring the baby up alone. I suspect that she will be only too pleased to take a financial incentive in exchange for the baby. Clearly having a baby was a whim and the reality of life as a single parent has proved less romantic than she expected.'

'I think you underestimate the attachment between a mother and her child,' Carlo said quietly. 'Especially a mother who went to the trouble of having artificial insemination in order to conceive. She would have had a counselling session at the clinic and her reasons for wanting a child must have been good. I doubt that she will give the baby up lightly.'

'You're wrong.'

'Maybe.' Carlo gave a brief smile. 'But my advice is stick to mending hearts, and leave the serious business of baby-making to those of us with some understanding of the emotions involved.'

'I understand the emotions better than most.' Nico's teeth were gritted and Carlo gave a sigh.

'*Sì*, I know you do.'

Nico shrugged, his black eyes hard and cold. 'Then you'll understand why I am right to go after the baby.'

'I understand, but I don't condone it.' Carlo picked up the file again. 'Answer me one question. If Abby Harrington had turned out to be in her late thirties and happily married, would you be threatening to take the baby?'

Nico frowned as if the question was completely superfluous. 'Of course not. I would have checked that they had everything they needed and walked away.'

But it would have been the hardest thing he'd ever had to do in his life.

'Then do the same thing now,' Carlo said quietly. 'You cannot take a child from its mother. Let it go, Nico. If you want family life, find a nice girl and marry her.'

Nico's eyes were hooded. 'Like you have, you mean?'

'I'm still auditioning for the role.' Carlo's dark eyes flashed wickedly and Nico raised an eyebrow in mockery.

'You feel the need to audition the whole female population?'

Carlo gave a rueful smile. 'All right, I'm the first to admit that, like you, I've never found a woman who can see further than my wallet.' His smile faded. 'But that fact doesn't make this right, Nico, and you know it.'

'I'm not seeking your approval.' Nico's tone was harsh. 'I came here because I wanted the answer to a question.'

'Which was?'

'I wanted to know if you were aware of her deception.'

Carlo shook his head. 'No. I didn't deal with her case and you should know me well enough to know that I wouldn't do that to you.'

Nico's expression darkened. 'Lucia did.'

Carlo shrugged. 'As we both know, Lucia is young and impulsive. And very spoilt by our parents. This was probably another one of her whims.' He walked towards his brother and laid a hand on his shoulder. 'I know you don't take advice from anyone, but I'm going to give it anyway. Whatever reasons this girl had for deceiving us, she clearly wanted that child. Don't jump to conclusions. Are you absolutely sure she knows you're the father?'

'Of course she knows.' Nico was back in control, his

emotions buried under the icy exterior for which he was renowned. 'Lucia told me at the time that her friend drew up a list of qualities that she wanted in a father and I was the perfect match.'

His tone was bitter and Carlo sighed.

'Lucia adores you, Nico. She probably genuinely did think you'd be the best father in the world and you know that all her school friends worshipped you. She just didn't think it through.'

Nico's mouth tightened. 'She never thinks things through.'

'And as for the friend—if she does know, she clearly didn't want you to find out.' Carlo rubbed a hand across the back of his neck, clearly concerned. 'This is going to come as a shock to her, Nico.'

Nico's mouth tightened. 'Good.'

Abigail Harrington had deceived him. She was clearly a calculating, manipulative woman who was totally unsuited to motherhood. As far as he was concerned, the bigger the shock, the better.

CHAPTER ONE

'I HATE leaving her—she was a bit fretful in the night. I'm afraid she might be coming down with something.' Abby reluctantly handed her daughter over to Karen, the nursery nurse who ran the hospital crèche. 'Maybe I should have kept her at home, but they're so short-staffed on the ward that I just couldn't do it to them, and—'

'Abby, stop worrying!' Karen interrupted her gently and settled Rosa on her hip, her expression sympathetic and mildly amused. 'She looks perfectly healthy to me. I know you feel guilty about working but you don't need to. There are plenty of single mothers in the world and plenty of them have to work. She has a really great time here and you're a brilliant mother. The best I know.'

Was she?

Abby bit her lip, painfully aware that Karen didn't know the whole truth of Rosa's conception.

It was a part of her life that she never discussed with anyone.

And although it was true that there were plenty of single mothers in the world, there were surely very few in her situation. And because she never forgot that she'd chosen this life for Rosa, she was doubly determined to be the very best mother that she could be.

'It's so hard for you, being on you own. You must feel so lonely sometimes,' Karen said gently. 'I know you don't like talking about it, but do you ever think of contacting her father?'

'No.' Abby shook her head.

How could she? Because she'd been so desperate to have a baby, she'd chosen to do so without the traditional support of a man. Rosa's conception had been arranged with clinical efficiency and total secrecy, and she had absolutely no idea who the father was.

And that knowledge nagged at her constantly despite the fact that the pain of her own childhood had left deep scars and she was only too aware that having two parents was no guarantee of childhood bliss. She'd been sent to boarding school at the age of seven by workaholic parents keen to relieve themselves of a child they'd never wanted, so she knew better than anyone that two parents didn't necessarily make a happy family.

But that didn't stop her feeling guilty that she'd deprived Rosa of a father.

'You never talk about it and you're always so self-contained and independent.' Karen sighed. 'He must have hurt you so much.'

Abby bit her lip, unable to correct the misconception without giving away her secret. The truth was that Rosa's father hadn't hurt her at all. *She didn't even know him.* All she knew was what her friend Lucia had told her. That the donor was Italian and very clever. And as for being independent, well, she'd had to be. Unlike most of her peers, her parents had never been there for her so she'd learned to take care of herself.

'How's little Thomas Wood?' Karen settled Rosa more comfortably on her hip and changed the subject neatly. 'When's he going for his op?'

'Tomorrow.' Abby pulled a face and handed over a bag containing all Rosa's things for the day. 'That's the other reason I felt I had to work today. I need to give his parents some support. They're terrified.'

'I'm not surprised.' Karen shook her head, her expression sombre. 'I can't begin to imagine how it must feel to see your five-month-old baby going for open-heart surgery.'

'Yes.' Abby leaned forward to kiss her daughter one more time. 'Still, Thomas is luckier than some. We've got an Italian surgeon arriving today to spend a few months on the unit until they appoint someone permanently. He's supposed to be one of the best there is and he's going to be teaching and working on the wards for a while. He's doing Thomas's operation. With an audience of thousands, from what I can gather. I hope he's got steady hands.'

She stroked a hand over Rosa's head, marvelling at how silky her dark hair was. 'You promise to call me if you're worried about her? Even if she's just a bit off colour—'

'For crying out loud, Abby!' Karen gave her an exasperated look and waved a hand towards the door. 'Just go, will you? She'll be fine!'

Abby gave a faltering smile, cast a last longing look at her daughter and then forced herself to leave the brightly decorated crèche and make her way up to the paediatric surgical ward where she worked. As usual she had a dull ache in the pit of her stomach.

She hated leaving Rosa so much.

It was like a physical wrench that didn't seem to get any easier with time. Given the chance, she would have spent every moment of every day just playing with her daughter and cuddling her but circumstances made that impossible. She *had* to work. Fortunately she loved her job and knew how lucky she was to work on such a respected unit. She found the field of paediatric cardiac surgery stimulating and absorbing and she knew that once she arrived on the ward she'd put thoughts of Rosa to one side and concentrate instead on the sick children and worried parents who needed her care.

And in a way Karen was right, she reassured herself firmly as she pressed the button for the lift. Plenty of parents worked and their children didn't suffer for it.

She took comfort from the fact that Rosa was a happy, sociable child and being with the other children in the crèche provided her with an important source of stimulation.

As the lift doors opened she straightened her uniform and checked that her long blonde hair was securely fastened.

'Hi, Abby.' Heather, the ward sister, greeted her with a warm smile and gestured towards the side room. 'The Woods are biting their nails to the quick in there. Fortunately we're well staffed today so you should be able to concentrate on them and give them all the support they need.' She glanced around furtively and lowered her voice. 'And maybe you'd better check they understand everything that's happening. Mr Forster had a brief chat with them before he left but you know what he was like, poor thing. He never had any time for the parents and he was hopeless at explaining anything. They looked more confused when he came out than they did when he went in.'

Abby gave a wry smile. One of their consultants, Mr Forster, had just taken early retirement on the grounds of ill health, but it was widely rumoured that he had just been finding the job too stressful. It was certainly true that he'd always been hopeless at explaining. He used the same terminology that he used with his medical team so his patients never understood him. 'Perhaps the new surgeon will set an example.'

'Let's hope so. Thomas should be first on the list tomorrow and our Italian whiz-kid should be up later to talk to them.'

Abby's blue eyes gleamed with amusement. 'Whiz-kid' seemed a strange description for someone with such an awesome reputation who was doubtless crusty and grey-haired. She'd never met the man in question but she was sure that he'd long ago outgrown the 'whiz-kid' title.

Making her way to the side room, she tapped on the door and walked in.

Lorna Wood had Thomas on her lap and he was dozing quietly.

'Hi, there.' Abby's voice was hushed so that she didn't disturb the baby and Lorna looked up, her face pale.

'Oh, Abby, I'm so pleased to see you.'

'How are you doing?'

Not very well, by the look of her, but, then, that was hardly surprising in the circumstances. Abby couldn't begin to imagine how she'd feel if it was Rosa who was about to have major heart surgery.

Lorna pulled a face. 'I feel awful. Worried, panicky...' She spoke in an undertone, careful not to wake the sleeping baby. 'But mostly I feel guilty.'

'Guilty?' Abby's eyebrows rose in surprise and she closed the door behind her. 'Why guilty?'

The young mother shrugged helplessly. 'Because Thomas seems fine most of the time and I'm asking myself if all this is necessary. Am I doing the right thing by letting him have the op?' Lorna glanced at her, her eyes filling as she begged for answers. 'I know they keep telling me that he'll get worse, but why not wait until it happens? Why do the operation now?'

More evidence that Mr Forster's explanations had been less than perfect, Abby thought, hoping that the new consultant would have a better way with words. With Mr Forster they'd virtually had to provide a translation.

'I know that Thomas seems well, but waiting might damage the heart further,' she said quietly, and Lorna bit her lip.

'But how do we know that for sure?'

Abby took her hand and gave it a squeeze. 'I think you need to talk it through with the surgeon who is going to do the operation,' she suggested. 'He's coming to see Thomas later. I'll make sure that he knows that you're worried so that he finds time to answer your questions.'

Clearly, concisely and in language that could be understood by normal mortals!

Lorna shrank slightly in her seat. 'I don't want to bother

him,' she said quickly. 'He's an important man and I'm the least of his worries.'

'You won't be bothering him,' Abby said firmly, used to dealing with that type of attitude. She'd lost count of the times patients had told her they refrained from asking questions because they didn't want to bother the doctor. 'If there are things you don't understand then you must ask!'

Lorna pulled a face. 'I find doctors really intimidating. Especially surgeons who can operate on a child's heart.' Her eyes were round with admiration. 'I mean, can you imagine being clever enough to do something like that? I always feel as though my questions are stupid and I'm wasting their time. Mr Forster has explained everything to me once. It isn't his fault if I'm too stupid to understand.'

'You're not stupid, Lorna,' Abby said firmly, making a mental note to brief the new consultant fully. He needed to spend time with the Woods. And he needed to use simple language. 'If it would make you feel better, I'll make sure I'm there, too. And I'll make sure that he doesn't leave the room until you've asked him every question you have and fully understand what's happening.'

'This whole thing feels like a nightmare. I just wish this was all a dream and I could wake up,' Lorna muttered, and Abby leaned forward and gave her a quick hug.

'The worst part is the waiting.' She looked at the sleeping child and smiled. 'I need to do his obs—you know, temperature, pulse that sort of thing—but I'll wait for him to wake up. Later on I want to take you to the cardiac intensive care unit—we call it CICU—so that you know what to expect when Thomas comes back from Theatre.'

Lorna bit her lip. 'Is it very scary?'

'It can seem scary,' Abby said, her tone gentle. She knew how important it was to be honest with parents and to prepare them for what lay ahead. 'You know that when he first comes back from Theatre he'll have a tube down his throat to help him breathe and a drain in his chest, as well as a drip. The monitors can seem very high-tech and daunting but the staff on CICU are wonderful and I know they'll take good care of you and Thomas. We've a baby who has just had a similar operation to Thomas on the unit at the moment so I can show you what to expect and you can chat to the parents.'

'And after CICU he'll come back here to the ward?'

'Once the doctors feel he's well enough, they'll transfer him back here.'

Lorna cuddled the sleeping child closer. 'And will you still be the nurse looking after us? You're always so calm. Nothing seems to make you flap—the minute you walk into the room I feel less panicky. I don't think I could bear having anyone else.'

'When I'm on duty I'll be your nurse,' Abby assured her. 'We try and maintain continuity whenever we can.'

Lorna gave a weak smile. 'Our nurse. You're supposed to be Thomas's nurse but you end up looking after the whole family.'

'That's because the whole family is part of Thomas's recovery,' Abby pointed out gently.

The whole ethos of the ward was to give care to the whole family, in recognition of the stress on the parents when a child was undergoing major surgery.

'Give me a call when Thomas wakes up and I'll check his obs,' she said, picking up his chart and checking what had happened in the night. 'In the meantime, I'll track down this new consultant and make sure he makes time to see you.'

'I hear that he's Italian.' Lorna looked at her anxiously. 'Is he good, Abby?'

Abby thought of the eulogies that had been heaped on the man's head in the past few weeks and smiled.

'He's better than good, Lorna. The doctors here say that he's a legend in paediatric cardiac surgery. He's pioneered several different techniques and his results are astonishing.

That's why he's going to spend some time over here wit
us. Sharing his experience as well as filling in for M
Forster until they make a permanent appointment. It hap
pens quite often, believe me. In a way Thomas is lucky tha
he's taken his case.'

Lorna nodded and gave a wan smile. 'I just hope he'
as good as you say.'

They shared a look of understanding, each knowing that
even in the most capable hands, operating on a child's hear
always carried a risk. The challenge was balancing the ris
of the operation with the risk of not correcting the defec
in the heart.

It was midmorning when there was a sudden bustle on th
ward and a group of doctors arrived, looking round expec
tantly.

'Is Mr Santini here yet?' Greg Wallis, the surgical reg
istrar, glanced into the office and Abby shook her head.

'If you mean the new consultant, no, not yet—he's bee
meeting the team on CICU and he's due here any minute.
She frowned slightly and looked at Greg. Had she hear
correctly? 'What did you say his name was again?'

'Santini. Domenico Santini. Why?'

Abby shook her head slightly. *It couldn't be…*

'I knew a Domenico Santini once,' she said lightly. '
went to school with his sister. But it can't be him. He'd b
too young.'

'Oh, this guy is young,' Greg told her, a trace of bitter-
ness in his voice. 'I used to think my career was going wel
until I read his CV. His rise to stardom had been positivel
meteoric. The guy is a genius by all accounts. His nicknam
in the theatre is ''Iceberg'' because he's the coolest surgeo
anyone has ever seen.'

Abby felt her heart thud uncomfortably in her chest
Could it be him? Lucia's brother?

As an impressionable young teenager she'd been thoroughly in awe of her friend's older brother. She was well aware that he was considered the ultimate catch by all the other girls in the school but on the few occasions that she'd met him she'd found him monumentally intimidating.

Fortunately he'd never even known that she existed.

She gave a slight smile at her own expense.

And why should he have noticed her? She'd been an awkward, leggy, painfully shy teenager with a brace on her teeth, glasses and hair that never behaved itself. There had been absolutely nothing about her that had been memorable. Especially compared to her peers.

The exclusive Swiss school which had been her home from the age of sixteen had attracted the children of the rich and famous from all over the world. Appeasing their consciences by selecting what they'd seen as the best, her parents had somehow found the money to send her there without considering whether Abby would fit in socially.

For the first term she'd been utterly miserable and painfully conscious of the differences in circumstances between her and the other girls.

She'd tried to shrink into the background to avoid attention and if it hadn't been for the flamboyant and boisterous Lucia Santini, her schooldays would have been a nightmare. As it was, the Italian girl had befriended her and made her life just about bearable.

Shocked that Abby's parents never visited, Lucia frequently invited Abby to stay with her own family but Abby declined, too awkward and embarrassed to accept hospitality which she knew she could never repay.

She also refused Lucia's invitations to join her on trips out with her older brother, knowing that such an outing would have been social torture. She never knew what to say to men anyway, let alone a man like Lucia's dark and dangerous brother. She must have been the only girl in the school that didn't try to attract his attention. Totally overwhelmed by his aggressive masculinity and cool self-confidence, Nico Santini made her thoroughly nervous. Carlo, the younger of the two brothers, seemed slightly more approachable, which was why she agreed to go to him for help so many years later.

She gave a sudden frown as an uncomfortable thought occurred to her.

Would the Santini family have discussed Rosa? Could Nico be aware of Rosa's history?

Greg cast her an odd look. 'Are you all right? You've gone really pale.'

'I'm fine,' she muttered, flashing him a wan smile and giving herself a sharp talking-to.

There was no way he could know. Everything that happened at the clinic was confidential, she assured herself. And even if Lucia had been so indiscreet as to mention it to her older brother, there was no reason why he should be in the slightest bit interested in her life.

It was highly unlikely that he'd even remember who she was.

Applying logic and reason but still feeling uneasy, she gave a start as the ward doors opened again and Dr Gibbs, the paediatric cardiologist, walked briskly down the corridor, accompanied by the rest of the team and a tall, powerfully built stranger.

Abby recognised him immediately and against her will her stomach flipped over as her eyes skimmed over the broad shoulders and long, muscular legs. Nico Santini had always been breathtakingly good-looking, but maturity had given his looks a lethal masculine quality which had a critical effect on her pulse rate.

Which just proved that, despite her protestations to the contrary, she was as shallow as the next woman, she thought with a resigned sigh.

But maybe it wasn't entirely her fault.

The man was devastating.

There were five male doctors in the group but he drew

the eye, not just because of his impressive physique but because of the air of cool command which he wore with the same effortless ease as his impeccably cut grey suit.

Nico Santini was more of a man than any other male she'd ever met and Abby felt her face flush slightly as she scanned his handsome features.

Iceberg.

The description suited him, she thought wryly, remembering just how cool and in control the man had been even in his twenties. Lucia had adored her older brother but she'd also been more than a little afraid of him.

Observing from a safe distance, Abby had always believed that he was very hard on Lucia who could certainly be a bit silly sometimes but had a very kind heart.

She hadn't seen him for at least six years.

Would he recognise her? Should she say something?

She almost laughed aloud at the thought. He absolutely would not recognise her and there was no way she was going to say anything. The mere thought was laughable.

Hello, remember me? I was the shy little mouse at school with your sister who never said a word whenever you were around....

Jack Gibbs was introducing him to everyone and finally it was Abby's turn and she lifted her chin and met that penetrating dark gaze head on, determined not to be intimidated.

Reminding herself that she was now a grown woman with a child, she forced herself to look composed, at least on the outside, and held out a hand.

It was a mistake.

Just touching those long, strong fingers was like connecting with a powerful electric force field and she felt her insides tumble unexpectedly.

'Abby is one of our best paediatric nurses,' Jack was saying, his expression warm, 'and we're very lucky to have her. When everyone else is in a panic you can rely on Abby to be the voice of calm. She has an amazing way with the children and the parents. We doctors fight over her. If we have something difficult to say to a family then we make sure we have Abby with us.'

Startled by the praise and unsettled by Nico Santini's unrelenting grip on her hand, Abby gave Jack a fleeting smile and took a step backwards, deliberately removing her hand from the pressure of those long fingers.

'I'll remember that.' He spoke in a deep, masculine purr that held just a hint of an Italian accent. Not enough to cloud his enunciation but just enough to make his voice unbearably sexy. 'Are you the nurse who is looking after the Wood family?'

Abby nodded, wishing that he didn't have such a powerful effect on her. She hated the fact that she was as vulnerable to his particular brand of scorching masculinity as the rest of her sex. She would have given anything to have been indifferent to him.

Not wanting to dwell on the effect he had on her, Abby quickly turned to the subject of work.

'His mother is very worried and has lots of questions, but she's afraid to ask them. I think it would be helpful if you could find time to talk to her.' The expression in her blue eyes was slightly challenging as they met his. From the little she knew of him it was highly unlikely that he would have the time or the skills to show much sensitivity to parents.

'Why is she afraid to ask them?'

His brusque question took her by surprise. 'She thinks you're very busy and doesn't want to disturb you.'

'Does she now?' He held her gaze for a long moment, his lush, dark lashes shielding his expression. 'Then we must make sure that she has all the time she needs.'

Against her will, Abby's eyes dropped to his firm mouth and she found herself remembering the rumour that had spread among the girls when she'd been at school.

That Nico Santini was a spectacular lover.

Shaken by her own thoughts, she looked away from him, her colour rising.

It was just the way that all women reacted to Nico Santini, she assured herself silently. He was much too powerful a personality to leave anyone feeling indifferent. At least she had more sense than to fall for him. She could admire him from a distance, but any more than that would have sent her running for cover.

Finally Nico's eyes left her and he turned to the rest of the doctors. 'I will see the baby and the parents straight away.'

Jack Gibbs, frowned slightly, clearly put out by that decision and by the fact that Nico had taken control. As paediatric cardiologist, all the children were referred to him initially and he very much considered it to be 'his' ward.

'But the teaching round… We were assuming…'

'If the mother has questions then I deal with those as a priority,' Nico said immediately, his tone discouraging any argument from those around him. 'In my experience it is counter-productive and cruel to leave the family worrying unnecessarily. It is important that they feel that we are all part of the same team. I'll do the teaching round when I have answered her questions and, of course, everyone is welcome. Until then I will see the family with just the nurse who cares for them.'

He looked expectantly at Abby who was having trouble hiding her surprise. Agreeing to see the family so quickly suggested a sensitivity that she hadn't thought him capable of.

'They're in the side ward,' she said quietly, and he gave a brief nod.

'Then let's go and talk to them. Has she signed a consent form or do I need to go through that with her?'

'Mr Forster did it before he left but I think she'd appreciate the chance to discuss the operation again,' she said tactfully, as she tapped on the door and walked into the room.

Nico Santini walked straight over to the parents and introduced himself.

'I will be your baby's doctor for the operation. Once you are discharged you will see Dr Gibbs again. With your permission I would like to examine Thomas, and then we will talk. I am sure you have many questions for me.'

'Well, yes, I suppose...' Lorna gave a nervous smile and clasped her hands in her lap. 'But I'm sure you're too busy for questions—'

'Not at all.' Nico gave her a warm smile which softened the harsh planes of his handsome face. 'At the moment I have nothing important to do,' he lied smoothly, 'and I am very happy to spend as long as you need in order to set your mind at rest. It's important to me that you don't worry. A worried mother means a worried baby and...' he raised his hands expressively '...I don't want either on my ward. Please, ask me anything you wish as many times as you need to. I understand that it can take a while to understand some of the things that we talk about. Hearts are complex things.'

Abby's jaw dropped and she struggled to hide her surprise as she listened to him talk. She'd always thought that Nico Santini was one hundred per cent alpha male. She hadn't imagined that there was a caring side to him.

But clearly there was.

She watched in fascination as he picked up Thomas with easy confidence, his hands swift and gentle as he examined the child. And all the time he spoke softly in Italian and the baby gazed up at him, his attention caught.

Even the baby can't look away from the man, Abby thought wryly, standing quietly in the background as Nico finally returned the baby to the cot and sat down next to Lorna.

'Please, feel free to ask me anything you wish.'

He inclined his dark head towards the young mother, listening closely as she blurted out all her worries. He was totally relaxed and attentive, nothing in his body language suggesting that there was a crowd of doctors waiting impatiently for him to finish so that he could do a teaching round.

'Tell me why you feel guilty.'

'He seems so well. I feel like a bad mother, deciding to make him have an operation that might—might…' Tears bloomed in Lorna Woods's eyes and Nico reached out and closed long fingers around her hand.

'It is clear to me that you haven't understood the explanations that you've been given so far and this is understandable. When a mother is told that her child is seriously ill, it is normal that she hears nothing more.' He shrugged a broad shoulder in a totally Latin gesture. 'I will explain, and you will ask me any questions you have. And then you will feel more reassured.'

Abby hid a smile. That was more like the Nico Santini she remembered. Accustomed to giving out orders.

You will be reassured or else…

Still, Lorna seemed to be hanging onto every word he said. And his hand.

'I just feel perhaps we should wait. I know he looks a bit blue but he doesn't seem that ill at the moment and I feel awful making him have this operation.'

Nico nodded, sympathy and understanding in his dark eyes. 'But you are not the one making the decision, Lorna. The doctors here have made the decision that Thomas needs this operation and you are being a good mother by agreeing to it.' He kept hold of her hand, his voice deep and level as he spoke. 'Thomas has something called Fallot's tetralogy, which basically means that there are a number of things wrong with his heart. Experience has shown us that if we delay the repair it puts a strain on one of the chambers of the heart. It can become enlarged and this may cause problems in later life. Also, repairing the fault early in life restores the oxygen saturation—the amount of oxygen in his blood. This is important for normal development.'

Lorna looked at her husband who shrugged his shoulders helplessly. 'So you really think it should be done now?'

'Definitely.' Nico didn't hesitate. 'I have reviewed all his tests and I am convinced that it is totally the right thing to do.'

Lorna nibbled her lip and looked at him shyly. 'Do you have children yourself?'

There was a long pause and Nico Santini glanced towards Abby, his dark lashes shielding his expression.

Confused by his sudden attention, she shifted slightly and felt herself colour.

Why was he looking at her?

He seemed to look at her for a long time and then finally he turned his attention back to Lorna. 'If you are asking if I would recommend this operation for my own child in the same situation, the answer is yes. I can assure you that if Thomas *were* my child, I would have no hesitation in letting the operation go ahead. Do you understand the actual mechanics of the operation? What I will be doing?'

Lorna blushed slightly and exchanged awkward glances with her husband. 'Sort of.'

Which meant no, Abby thought quickly, preparing to intervene. But Nico was ahead of her.

'Maybe I will explain it again,' he said smoothly, releasing Lorna's hand and reaching into his pocket for a pad and a pen. 'A drawing usually helps. Imagine the heart as four chambers…'

His pen moved quickly over the pad as he drew a diagram to illustrate his explanation.

'One of the problems with Thomas's heart is what we call a VSD—a ventricular septal defect. In other words, there is a hole between the two chambers here….' He tapped his pen on the page to demonstrate what he meant more clearly. 'I will put a patch on that. Here the artery is narrowed and I need to sort that out, probably by opening up the valve that leads into it.'

Nico continued his explanation and finally Lorna's husband gave a weak smile. 'You make it sound like DIY.'

Nico gave a brief nod. 'In a way it is. I am a technician. Only I don't always know exactly what will need to be done until I have a look at the heart.' He gave another shrug. 'You just have to trust me.'

Lorna bit her lip and he lifted an eyebrow.

'There is something else you wish to ask me?'

'You say we must trust you....' Lorna hesitated and then took a deep breath. 'Are you good?'

Nico seemed momentarily taken aback by the question and then he gave a wry smile and touched her cheek briefly with a long finger.

'The best.'

Abby stayed silent as Lorna visibly relaxed and started to ask all the questions that had clearly been bothering her for some time.

Finally she seemed happier and Nico rose to his feet in a fluid movement and flashed her a smile.

'I hope you feel a little better now.'

Lorna nodded and gave him a weak smile. 'I do feel better, thank you, although I can't pretend I'm not worried.'

'Of course you will be worried.' Nico slipped his pen back into his pocket. 'You are a mother and it is a mother's role to worry. If there are any other questions that you wish to ask me then just ask one of the nurses to contact me and I will be happy to speak to you at any time. I will come and find you after the operation tomorrow so that I can tell you how it went.'

At the reminder of what lay ahead, Lorna swallowed and he reached out a hand and squeezed her shoulder.

'It will go well. Trust me.'

With that he strode out of the room, leaving Abby to follow in his wake, stunned by what she'd witnessed.

It wasn't at all what she'd expected.

She'd never seen a doctor take so much time with a family before and she was impressed by how skilfully he'd translated the technical aspects of the operation into language that the family could understand. She was also impressed by the way he'd picked up the signals that Lorna hadn't understood the previous explanations that she'd been given.

Maybe she'd misjudged him.

'Thank you for giving them so much time. I've never heard a doctor give such a clear explanation. You were amazing with them,' she admitted quietly, as she walked back along the corridor beside him.

He stopped dead and turned to face her, a frown touching his forehead, almost as though he'd forgotten she was there until she'd spoken.

His eyes locked with hers and suddenly she remembered the way he'd looked at her in the side room.

Accusingly.

Which was utterly ridiculous, she told herself firmly. What could he possibly be accusing her of?

Or maybe he'd recognised her but couldn't place her.

Maybe she should tell him that she used to go to school with Lucia?

His gaze was cool and assessing and something in those fabulous dark eyes chilled her to the bone.

'Are you staying for my teaching round?'

'I can't.' She was off duty at four and nothing was going to stop her seeing Rosa. She'd nipped down to the crèche in her lunch-break to check that the baby was all right, but she'd be happier when they were both at home.

'And will you be at home this evening?' His voice was silky smooth and she nodded, taken aback by the question.

Why would Nico Santini be remotely interested in her plans for the evening?

His eyes scanned her face with disconcerting thoroughness and then he turned on his heel and walked back onto the main ward, leaving her staring after him, thoroughly confused.

Nico completed his teaching round and glanced at his watch.

'Are you busy this evening?' Jack Gibbs was clearly about to extend a social invitation and Nico was quick to make his excuses.

There was only one place he intended to be that evening, and that was confronting Abby Harrington. Incredibly skilled at interpreting body language, he'd instantly recognised her nervousness when they'd been introduced.

His mouth twisted into a bitter smile. After all these years he didn't think that he made mistakes about women, but he'd certainly been way off the mark in her case.

He'd thought her extremely shy, but she'd also seemed to him to be sensible and intelligent and he'd hoped that she might be a favourable influence on his dizzy sister. She certainly wasn't the sort of person he would have credited with telling lies or choosing to become a single mother.

It was no wonder she'd looked nervous when he'd walked onto the ward.

She was afraid that he'd discovered her secret and at this very moment she was probably pacing the floor of the tiny flat that she was being forced to vacate, dreading his next move.

And she was right to dread it.

Perfect father material.

Wasn't that what Lucia had said when she'd persuaded him to be the donor? That they'd decided that he had all the qualities that a man should have. Looks and intellect. Unfortunately for them, they'd failed to realise that being perfect father material also included a sense of responsibility towards fatherhood and it was that same sense of duty that had driven him to check on the child that he'd fathered.

He wondered how Abby Harrington would react when he announced that he intended to claim his child.

For some reason she'd wanted a child of her own and had clearly been prepared to use any means to achieve her objective. Including persuading his sister to lie about her circumstances, he reminded himself grimly.

She'd played a dangerous game and lost.

And now she was going to pay the price.

CHAPTER TWO

ABBY tucked Rosa into her cot and stared down at her with a worried frown. Her cheeks were pink and she'd been unusually fretful again during the evening.

Abby kept trying to convince herself that it was probably just teething, but all her instincts were telling her that the child was coming down with something.

She gave a sigh and stroked the little girl's hair as she slept.

She loved her so much...

The sound of the doorbell disturbed her and she glanced at the clock, her heart accelerating like a roller-coaster.

Was it the landlord?

He'd given her two more weeks to find somewhere else to live but so far she hadn't found the time to start hunting.

Remembering what had happened during their last encounter, her breathing grew more rapid and she glanced at the phone.

Should she call the police?

Surely it was illegal to double the rent just because the tenant had refused sex with the landlord!

The bell went again, more insistent this time, and she walked purposefully towards the door, sparks in her blue eyes.

She didn't need the police. This time she'd handle him herself. She didn't even care about the flat any more. It wasn't anything special and in the winter it was freezing. But she needed time to find somewhere else that she could afford and that was impossible in London. She already had to take two buses to get to work and if she moved further out then it would make the journey even worse and that wasn't fair on Rosa.

But if he tried what he'd tried last time…

Determined to ask for a bit more time, Abby jerked open the front door and gasped in surprise as she saw who was standing there.

It was Nico Santini.

What did he want?

And how had he known where to find her?

For a moment she didn't speak, too taken aback to think of anything sensible to say, then finally she found her voice.

'Well—this is a surprise…'

Instead of answering, he stepped past her and strode into her flat, ducking his dark head slightly to avoid banging his head on the doorway.

Abby's jaw dropped. The arrogance of the man!

Closing the front door behind her, she followed him into the shabby sitting room and paused in the doorway. He was standing with his back to her, his powerful shoulders tense as he examined a photograph.

A photograph of Rosa.

Abby bristled, outrage overwhelming her usual shyness. 'Did you want something?'

He didn't even look up, his dark eyes intent on the photograph.

Abby tensed. 'That's my daughter.'

He looked up then, his gaze lifting slowly from the photograph to meet her eyes. 'I know exactly who she is, Abby. I know everything about her.'

Everything?

What exactly did he mean, he knew *everything*?

She hid her dismay. What was he saying? That Lucia had told him about her treatment at Carlo's clinic?

She watched, struggling to think logically as he returned the photograph to the shelf with the others, his lean brown hand totally steady.

Why was Nico even interested? she wondered frantically. Why would her daughter be of interest to him? He'd never even passed the time of day with her before.

He took a final look at the photograph and then turned, supremely confident, every inch the arrogant, dominant male as he faced her across the sitting room.

Abby fought the instinct to take a step backwards. This was her sitting room, for goodness' sake.

But his self-assured masculinity stifled her powers of speech and she dug her fingers into her palms and took a deep breath. There was something about this man that punctured her confidence levels.

'Secrets have a way of coming out, Abby.' He spoke slowly, his voice loaded with meaning, and she started to shake.

He definitely knew.

'Let's not play games. It isn't my style. I assume you're referring to Rosa's conception,' she said flatly, deciding that pretence was clearly a waste of time. 'That should have been confidential but I suppose between siblings anything goes. What I don't understand is why you could possibly be interested.'

'No?' His black eyes glinted slightly and he tossed a file onto the small writing desk by the French doors that led into the tiny garden.

Abby glanced at it, startled, realising that she hadn't even noticed until now that he'd been carrying a file.

She stared at it now with trepidation, instinct telling her that the contents would be unpleasant.

'Wh-what is that?'

'Take a look,' he suggested, his tone lethally smooth, and she looked at him with a total lack of comprehension.

What was this all about?

Staring at the file as though it were a deadly animal which might strike at any moment, she forced herself to cross the room. It had a plain brown cover which revealed nothing of its contents.

Pausing momentarily, she lifted a hand and flipped it open and then jerked her hand away as if it had been scalded.

The file was about *her*!

Her and Rosa.

Her whole body trembling, she flicked through the pages, nausea rising in her throat as she read intimate details about herself and her daughter. Intimate and exhaustive details.

Details that no one should know.

An intensely private person, she felt painfully exposed, flayed by the knowledge that this man was in possession of such detailed facts about her.

Appalled, she lifted her eyes to his. 'H-how did you get this information?'

Nico lifted a broad shoulder dismissively. 'That isn't important.'

It was important to her. She'd always hidden the truth about Rosa's conception from those around her. And here it was staring up at her, taunting her from the page of a file delivered by a virtual stranger.

The fact that he knew about Rosa's history was bad enough, but to know every detail of her life…

She stared at him, seeking some clue as to the game he was playing, but he was everything that his reputation suggested. *Iceberg*. If he was feeling anything at all, it certainly didn't show. There was no doubt as to who had the upper hand, and it wasn't her.

'Why? Why are you interested in us?' Her words were barely a whisper, almost a plea, but there wasn't a glimmer of sympathy in those hard black eyes.

'*Dio*, you really ask me that? Are you still pretending that you don't know why I am here?' He walked purposefully towards her and when he finally came to a halt he was standing so close to her that she could feel the warmth from his powerful body. 'Did you really think I wouldn't find out the truth, Abby?'

'The truth about what?' She swallowed, her breathing shallow as she struggled to understand what was happening. She was obviously missing something. And whatever it was that she was missing, it was clearly something very serious.

'Are you really pretending that you don't know who I am?'

Her chin jerked up and she met his gaze. 'I know who you are.' Clearly she should have confessed straight away, but it just hadn't seemed that important and she'd thought it unlikely that he even would have remembered her. 'You're Lucia's brother. I met you a few times when we were at school.'

'And?' he prompted her softly, and she felt her heart hammering uncomfortably in her chest.

He hadn't even raised his voice but somehow his tone had filled her with dread.

'And nothing.' She looked at him helplessly, her fingers curled into her damp palms. 'I haven't seen you since we left school. I truly don't know what this is all about.'

'But you're not denying that you had treatment at my brother's clinic?' His tone was silky smooth, challenging her to dispute the truth.

'No.' She swallowed painfully, accepting the fact that he obviously had all the facts at his disposal. The file was nauseatingly comprehensive. 'What would be the point of that when you've gone to so much trouble to find out every last detail about me? But that information should have been confidential.'

His mouth tightened. 'And you were doubtless depending on that fact when you lied to us all. You were confident that you wouldn't be caught.'

'Lied?' Abby's eyes widened and she shook her head, totally confused by the conversation. It was like taking the lead part in a play when she hadn't read the script. 'I didn't lie to anyone.'

'Maybe not directly, but you were happy for Lucia to do it for you,' he said harshly. 'She lied about your age and your marital status.'

Abby blinked. 'No, I—'

He made an impatient sound. 'I have been intimately acquainted with your sex since I was fifteen years old and I can assure you that I am no longer taken in by a pair of wide blue eyes and an innocent expression. I know everything there is to know about female manipulation.'

Abby grabbed the back of a chair, shell-shocked. Nico was accusing her of something, but she still didn't understand what. He was making no sense at all.

'What am I supposed to have lied about?' She let go of the chair and hugged her arms around herself. 'I really don't know what this conversation is about.'

He stared at her, his black eyes merciless. 'No? Then let me spell it out.' He paced across her small sitting room and she couldn't help comparing him with a caged tiger. Only maybe a tiger would have been safer, she thought weakly. Nico in a rage was a lethal force. 'You played a dangerous game and you have lost.'

She stared at him stupidly, her powers of speech temporarily suspended by shock.

He barely seemed to notice her lack of communication. As far as he was concerned, she'd been tried and found guilty. The only problem was, she had absolutely no idea what crime she'd supposedly committed.

'I was willing to help you only because I believed your circumstances to be worthy of intervention. I have now found out otherwise and this changes everything.'

Was the man mad? When had he helped her?

She struggled to find her voice. 'Perhaps you should be more specific,' she croaked. 'What exactly does it change?'

'Everything. I no longer consider you a fit mother,' he

delivered in a cool tone. 'I agreed to father your child because I believed you to be a woman in your late thirties in a stable relationship with a limited chance of producing a child naturally. That was what you and Lucia led me to believe. The truth was very different, as we both know. I never would have agreed to be the donor had I known that you were so young and on your own.'

She stared at him blankly, her brain slower than her hearing. 'Donor?'

He ignored her croaked response.

'You are clearly not able to give her the type of care I would wish for a child of mine, so I intend to apply for custody myself. I want my child.'

His child?

Donor?

The world stopped dead and Abby stared at him in mute horror.

Nico Santini thought that he was Rosa's father?

She opened her mouth and then closed it again, unable to voice the words aloud because that might have given credence to his absurd claim. And it *was* absurd, of that she was sure.

'Don't bother denying it,' Nico drawled, but Abby wasn't listening. Her mind was locked on something he'd said a few sentences earlier.

Something about Lucia…

A hideous suspicion formed inside her mind and Abby lifted a hand to her head as she tried to clear the humming in her ears.

It was possible, just possible that…

Nausea rose in her throat and she reached out and grasped the bookshelves for support, but it made no difference. The room suddenly started to spin and she heard Nico swear softly in Italian.

'*Dio*, fainting will not attract my sympathy.'

Sympathy? She didn't want his sympathy. She just

wanted him to be lying!! And she wanted him out of her house.

'Sit down and put your head between your knees.' His voice was rough and before she could protest he'd scooped her up into his arms and dumped her unceremoniously into a chair. Then she felt his long fingers biting into the soft flesh at the back of her neck as he forced her head between her knees.

She gulped in air, trying desperately to control the nausea that threatened to engulf her.

Finally the blackness receded and she gingerly tried to sit up. 'You can move your hand now,' she muttered sickly, 'I'm fine.'

The pressure at the back of her neck eased and she sat up slowly, one palm placed across her chest. She needed to check that her heart was still beating.

Nico stood in front of her, his legs placed firmly apart in an aggressive stance, his expression brutally unsympathetic.

'I always thought Lucia took the prize when it came to drama, but it seems I was wrong. I hate to disappoint you but I'm never impressed by female hysterics,' he informed her. 'Even less so in your case since you've always known that I might find out the truth.'

Abby was forcing herself to breathe normally in an attempt to get oxygen to her fuddled brain.

Finally she felt well enough to speak. 'Are you really telling me that you think you're the father of my baby?'

Her voice sounded thick, clogged with emotion. Totally unlike her own.

'I don't *think*.' He spoke the words with dangerous emphasis. 'I *know*.'

Her voice was little more than a whisper. 'You were the donor?'

Please, let it be a mistake....

His black eyes flashed with impatience. 'You know very

well that I was. And we also know that you and Lucia fed me false information so that I'd agree. She knew that I would never agree to father a child for a woman in your circumstances. Family is something that I feel very strongly about. The two of you concocted the sort of story that you knew I would respond to.'

Abby licked dry lips. Was he telling the truth? Could Nico Santini be the father of her child?

She and Lucia had discussed the qualities that would make the ideal donor, but she'd never asked for any details.

What would have been the point? She'd assumed that the man in question would have been a stranger to her.

Had Lucia really persuaded her own brother to be the donor? Surely she never would have done that.

But if she had…

Abby sank her teeth into her lower lip, refusing to face the awful possibility that Nico might be Rosa's father.

It was too shocking even to contemplate. She could see instantly that a man like Nico, an Italian who'd had the sanctity of the family injected into his veins from the cradle, wasn't going to sit back and allow his child to be brought up by a single mother. What had Lucia been thinking of?

And he'd said something about taking Rosa from her.

The colour drained from her face and she lifted a hand to her mouth. She was going to be ill.

Muttering an apology, she stood up hastily and sprinted to the toilet where she was violently sick. For endless moments she hung over the bowl and then finally she sank onto the floor of the bathroom, her eyes closed, every muscle in her body aching from her body's physical reaction to Nico's shocking announcement.

She had no idea of how long she sat there. Time was of no consequence. All she could think of was the fact that he just might be Rosa's father. And if he was then he was going to claim her.

Her baby.

Panic swamped her like a tidal wave and she wrapped her arms around her body, trying to settle her churning stomach. She had to stay calm, she told herself, clutching her shaking knees to her tummy and gulping in a lungful of air. Nico was exceptionally clever and so emotionally controlled that if she didn't get a grip and concentrate, he'd run rings around her.

She was still wrestling for control when Rosa suddenly cried out.

Struggling to her feet, she splashed her face quickly and ran down the hall as fast as her shaking legs would allow.

Pushing open the door of Rosa's nursery, she stopped dead. Nico was standing there, speaking softly in Italian, Rosa held firmly against his shoulder. The little girl lifted a chubby hand and patted his blue-black jaw, gurgling with laughter and blowing bubbles.

Abby watched in dismay.

Did her daughter have no sense of self-preservation? She should have been behaving like the child from hell so that there was no way on this planet he'd want to take her away. Instead of which, Rosa was being her usual sweet-natured self and she could see that Nico was totally enchanted by the little girl.

He held her against his broad chest with one large hand while he used the other to tease the baby gently.

Abby shook her head in disbelief as she watched them together. What a contrast. There was no sign of the hard, ruthless, male who had been prowling around her sitting room only moments earlier. With the baby Nico was a different person—incredibly gentle, tolerant and mildly amused by her antics.

Looking at the two of them together, Abby felt her heart sink into her boots.

How had she not noticed it before?

Rosa was the spitting image of Nico. They had the same

jet-black hair, the same incredible dark eyes. Only the mouth was different. Rosa's mouth was a small rosebud whereas—Abby glanced at him and then glanced away quickly, her face suddenly hot—Nico's was tough and sensual, and it wasn't something that she wanted to focus on. Whichever way you looked at it, physically Rosa resembled Nico closely.

Which meant that he was probably telling the truth.

The realisation hit her in the pit of her stomach and she sank against the doorframe for support. Even if she'd been thinking of contesting his claim to be the child's natural father, one look at the two of them together would have been enough to make her realise the futility of such an exercise.

Suddenly Rosa noticed her mother and squirmed in Nico's hold, reaching out her chubby arms towards Abby.

Distraught and not thinking clearly, Abby pulled herself together enough to cross the room and take her daughter from him.

Just feeling the familiar warmth of Rosa's little body made her feel better. There was something so comforting about her innocent hug and the smell of her skin and hair.

'She's mine.' Not wanting to upset Rosa, she spoke quietly, but her voice quivered with passion and sincerity. 'She's always been mine. It doesn't matter if you're the biological father. You can't take her away from me.'

Her words were sheer bravado and she met his cool gaze, hopelessly out of her depth. She had no idea about the legalities of the situation and she couldn't afford to pay anyone to tell her, not with the present state of her finances. Surely no one would give him custody? But, then again, they probably would, she reflected miserably, hugging her daughter even closer. The Santini family was loaded. When Lucia had been at school it had been bodyguards and helicopters all the way. They had enough money to buy the entire legal system if necessary. Whereas she—she closed her eyes briefly as she faced the painful truth—didn't even have the money for one consultation with a lawyer. If she had then she probably would have already seen one about her unscrupulous landlord.

Rosa squirmed slightly in her hold and Nico looked at her, the expression in his eyes hidden by sinfully long thick black lashes. 'I refuse to discuss this in front of the child. Put her back in the cot and settle her.'

Knowing that he was right and feeling guilty that she was upsetting Rosa, Abby had no choice but to comply. She settled the little girl in the cot, tucking her favourite teddy in next to her.

Then, with a last look at her precious child, she left the bedroom door ajar and walked into the tiny sitting room.

Nico walked in behind her and closed the door behind him with an ominous click.

'Now we can talk.'

If only it was that easy.

Painfully shy and a pacifist by nature, she'd always hated confrontation of any sort and in this case who could blame her? There was surely no one on the planet that would willingly choose Nico Santini as an adversary.

Even Lucia had been wary and nervous of her older brother and, facing him across the room, Abby could understand why. Nico just exuded masculine power and he clearly wasn't used to hearing the word 'no'.

But he was going to hear it now.

Abby folded her arms across her stomach and tried not to focus on just how anxious he made her feel. She'd never been comfortable with his raw, animal sexuality and nothing had changed over time. She was just a normal, everyday sort of girl and a complete novice when it came to handling men, whereas he—she swallowed as she risked a glance at his impressive male physique—was in a different league entirely.

Sophisticated, vastly experienced with women and used

to getting his own way in everything, he was just about as different from her as it was possible to be.

She tightened her fists by her side and lifted her chin. She might be nervous of him, but this was Rosa they were talking about.

Her baby.

Rosa was all she had in the world and he wanted to take her away.

Well, she wasn't going to allow that to happen, which meant standing up to him—whatever that took.

Maybe if she didn't look at him directly, he would seem less intimidating.

'I accept that you might be her father,' she conceded, proud by how steady her voice sounded. 'She certainly looks like you, but you have to believe that I knew nothing about it. I never would have wanted you to be the father!'

In fact, the mere thought that they'd been so intimately connected, albeit in such a clinical and detached way, made her feel hot inside.

Faint colour touched her cheek and she dipped her head forward, concentrating on the threadbare carpet. This whole situation was a total nightmare!

'You expect me to believe that?' His incredulous tone mocked her and she realised, helplessly, how utterly implausible she sounded.

She knew from Lucia that her brother had been chased by almost every female on the planet. Why should he possibly believe that there might be one who *didn't* see him as the perfect mate?

Nico Santini had everything. Intelligence, wealth, looks and power. He was the oldest son of one of the most powerful families in Italy, but he'd chosen not to enter the family business and instead had forged a staggeringly successful career as a heart surgeon. By all accounts the man was nothing short of a genius in the operating theatre. Who wouldn't want him to father her child? He was perfect father material for most women.

But she wasn't most women, she thought miserably, lacing her fingers in front of her in a nervous gesture.

She didn't respond to his full-on, testosterone-driven masculinity—it made her feel shivery and uncomfortable and strange inside. But, most importantly, for all his sense of family and responsibility, Nico Santini was a workaholic like her father and she knew only too well what it felt like to be the child of someone like that. A man like Nico would never have time for fatherhood.

She was still trying to find a tactful and convincing way to tell him that when he made an impatient sound.

'All right—let's leave that to one side for a moment and move on to the other issue. Your age. Lucia told me that you were in your late thirties, which was why I agreed to help.'

Abby shook her head, stunned into silence by the news that Lucia had told such lies.

'What I want to know is why a woman of twenty-two with no emotional or financial support from anyone would choose to have a child on her own.'

Abby's heart twisted.

How could she possibly tell him the truth? Nico came from a big, loving Italian family. How could a man like him even begin to understand what it felt like to be totally alone in the world, to have absolutely no one to laugh and cry with? How could he possibly understand what it felt like to be so achingly lonely that her idea of winning the lottery was to find a long-lost relative.

They probably didn't even have a word for lonely in the Italian language.

And she certainly wasn't confessing the details of her humiliating experience with Ian—

What would have been the point?

Lucia had always complained that her brother never let emotion interfere with any decision he made.

How could he begin to understand what had driven her to have a child of her own at such a young age, and how would she convince him that she hadn't taken the decision lightly?

She'd questioned herself long and hard before she'd finally decided to have a child, and that questioning hadn't ended with Rosa's birth. She was painfully conscious that she'd become a single mother through choice and that her decision had deprived Rosa of certain things in life.

Like a father.

But apart from that one factor, which persistently nagged at her conscience, she refused to believe that Rosa was badly off. She had a mother who adored her, which was more than many children had.

It was certainly more than she'd ever had herself.

Aware that Nico was looking at her with ill-concealed impatience, she forced herself to answer.

'I just wanted a baby.' It sounded lame even to her, and his mouth tightened.

'So you had one, with no thought to her future.'

'No!' Stung by the contempt in his tone, Abby forgot to be intimidated and lifted her head to look at him, her blue eyes blazing. 'I thought long and hard before I had Rosa. And I give her everything I have!'

'Which isn't very much, is it, *cara mia*?'

His softly spoken words were so cruel that she gave a gasp of disbelief.

'A happy childhood doesn't have to be about money.'

'Agreed.' He was ice cool, completely unfazed by her heated defence. 'But, correct me if I'm wrong, generally speaking a baby does need a stable home in which to live.'

Her heart started to beat faster. 'Rosa has a home!'

His dismissive glance round her tiny flat spoke volumes. 'One which you are being forced to leave.'

She stared at him, eyes wide. She hadn't told anyone about her accommodation problems.

'H-how do you know that?'

'I have impressive contacts.' He met her stunned gaze without a flicker of emotion. 'I'm intrigued as to how you are planning to give Rosa this "happy childhood" that you talk about when you don't have anywhere for her to live.'

Abby lifted her small chin. 'I'll find somewhere.'

'You wouldn't be leaving this place had you managed to keep up with the rental payments,' Nico pointed out smoothly, and she gasped.

He must have spoken to the landlord, and he'd obviously told him that she couldn't afford the rent.

She closed her eyes briefly and gritted her teeth. She'd done nothing wrong. The truth was that the landlord was totally corrupt. Unfortunately she had absolutely no experience in dealing with his type. He'd been pestering her for months and when she'd refused to give him what he wanted he'd increased her rent, knowing that she was already stretched to the limit on her modest nurse's salary. So now she was being forced to move out.

Pride prevented her from communicating the facts to Nico. It clearly suited his purposes to believe that she was a useless mother.

'You can't seriously want to take Rosa from me,' she said, her voice choked as she tried to reason with him. 'You're not even married. Why would you want a baby?'

He stilled, his powerful shoulders visibly tense. Abby watched him, intrigued in spite of her inner panic, her attention caught by the subtle change in him. So Nico Santini wasn't always an iceberg, she mused silently.

'I am in a position to give her a good life—'

'By whose definition?' Abby shot back, her shyness buried under the threat of losing Rosa. 'You're a workaholic. When do you have time for a child? Or are you planning to get married…?' Her voice trailed off at that awful thought. If he *was* getting married, he'd be a more appealing prospect for a judge, wouldn't he?

His dark eyes were veiled, any hint of emotion carefully concealed. Whatever had caused the tension moments earlier was now firmly buried again. 'I am not getting married.'

Belatedly Abby recalled conversations with Lucia. His sister had clearly said that her brother had never been emotionally attached to a woman in his life.

'He's never met a woman who didn't have an ulterior motive,' Lucia had told her once. 'They're either after his money or the status of being seen with him. It's the same with Carlo. Neither of them trust women an inch and frankly I don't really blame them.'

'Well, if you're not getting married, you're not in a position to give her a better home than I can,' Abby said, her voice shaking with passion. 'She's my baby and I won't let you take her!'

She had the satisfaction of seeing him look taken aback. In all probability no one had ever said 'no' to the man before. Well, tough, she thought. He'd better get used to the idea.

He opened his mouth to speak but then cursed softly as his mobile phone rang.

He reached into his pocket and flipped it open. 'Santini.' His voice was clipped, his face expressionless as he listened to the person on the other end. Then he issued some complex instructions and glanced at his watch. 'I will be there in ten minutes.'

He slipped the phone back into his pocket and a ghost of a smile played around his firm mouth.

'It looks like the rest of this conversation will have to wait until another time. One of the babies that was operated on yesterday has started to haemorrhage. I may need to take her back to Theatre.'

For a brief moment Abby forgot about her own problems. 'Which baby?'

'Katherine Parker.'

Abby gave a gasp and covered her mouth with her hand. 'No—not Katherine. That baby is so precious. They tried for ten years to have her—ten years…'

'Every baby is precious,' Nico said as he reached for the doorhandle. 'Which is why they deserve the security of a stable family. But we'll talk about that another time.'

Abby wasn't even thinking of her own problems any more. She was thinking about little Katherine and how devastated her parents would be. The operation had seemed to go so well.

'I hope you can save her,' she muttered, and he gave a cool shrug.

'I certainly intend to try.'

With that he tugged open the door and left her staring after him, trembling from the aftershock of the confrontation.

Crossing Nico Santini was like being caught in the eye of a hurricane. And it was far from over.

CHAPTER THREE

ALL the talk on the ward the next morning was about Katherine and the fact that Nico Santini had saved her.

'No wonder they call him "Iceberg". He opened her chest on CICU, cool as a cucumber,' Fiona said in an awed tone. 'I mean, can you imagine that? Apparently they wanted to take her to Theatre but he took one look at her and opened her up there and then.'

'Did he?' Abby was thrilled that the little girl was once again out of the woods, but all this hero-worship of Nico was making her feel slightly ill. Remembering the cool way in which he'd delivered his threats the night before, she wasn't exactly able to join the others in their adulation of the visiting consultant.

He might be a god in the operating theatre, but as far as she was concerned as a human being he left a great deal to be desired.

He seemed incapable of understanding normal human emotions.

Like the love of a mother for her child.

Fiona was looking at her closely. 'Are you all right? You're very pale. Did Rosa keep you up last night?'

Abby shook her head. After Nico had left, Rosa had slept right through the night, but she hadn't even attempted to sleep she'd been so anxious about the future.

Could he do as he'd threatened?

Could he take Rosa away from her?

She really ought to consult a lawyer but she wouldn't know whom to contact and it would mean admitting that Rosa had been conceived by donor insemination.

'I just feel a bit tired.' She managed a wan smile and

glanced at the clock on the wall. 'Little Thomas will be going down to Theatre in an hour—I'm going to check they're all right.'

Fiona walked along the corridor with her. 'Did you take them around CICU yesterday?'

Abby nodded, stroking a wild strand of pale blonde hair behind her ear. 'But you know how hard it is to make CICU seem anything less than scary. All those tubes and bleeping machines are enough to scare anyone.'

'Well, at least it's Nico Santini doing the operation. If it were my baby, there isn't anyone else I'd rather have after seeing what he did for Katherine,' Fiona said fervently, and Abby gave a half-smile, mildly amused by the other girl's attitude.

It was just as well she didn't know what he was really like.

'He's just a man, Fiona.'

Her colleague gave a cheeky grin. 'Oh, believe me, I've noticed. In fact, Heather has said I can go into Theatre this morning to watch him operate. I'm hoping that I don't faint.'

'Since when did you faint at the sight of blood?'

'It's not the sight of blood that's going to make me faint,' Fiona breathed, 'it's the sight of the surgeon. He's devastating.'

Abby looked at Fiona as if she'd grown horns. It was true that Nico was very good-looking, but he was also a control freak who had the emotional sensitivity of a wounded tiger.

She certainly wouldn't contemplate a relationship with a man like that that. But, then, her track record with relationships hadn't been exactly impressive, she reminded herself sadly.

Which was why she'd resorted to such extreme means to have a child of her own.

'Are you seriously telling me you don't find him attractive?' Fiona shot her a look of disbelief and Abby forced another smile.

'I can see that some women might find him handsome,' she said through stiff lips, 'but he isn't really my type.'

'Well, in that case don't ever introduce me to your type,' Fiona commented as they reached the door to the side ward. 'I'm off to see the man in action now. See you later.'

Abby watched her go and then walked quietly into the room. Thomas was lying in his cot, chuckling and playing with a rattle. His parents were sitting next to him, white-faced and clearly stressed. At the sight of Abby, Lorna shot to her feet.

'Are they ready for him?'

Abby gave her a gentle smile and shook her head. 'Not yet. Did you manage to get any sleep at all?'

'Not much.' Lorna bit her lip and twisted her hands together anxiously. 'I know that Nico said I could go with him to the operating theatre and stay with him until he'd had the anaesthetic, but I just don't think I can do that.'

Her voice was little more than a whisper and Abby gave her a hug. 'Lots of mothers find it too stressful, don't worry about it. Either your husband can go or I'll go with him.'

Lorna sniffed. 'He does know you and he likes you. Would you do it? Would you stay with him? I've given him a cuddle and said everything I need to say. If I go with him I know I won't be able to control myself and I don't want to upset him.'

'Of course I'll go.'

At that moment Heather put her head round the door to say that they were ready for Thomas in Theatre.

Lorna and her husband gave him a last cuddle and Abby felt her eyes fill with tears as she imagined the worry they must be feeling. At that particular moment she didn't care how arrogant Nico Santini was as long as he was able to operate successfully on Thomas.

In the anaesthetic room the anaesthetist chatted away to

her, but she barely heard him, her heart in her mouth as the doors through to Theatre swung open and Nico strolled through. He seemed impossibly broad-shouldered, his dark hair obscured by a cap and a hint of curling dark chest hair showing at the neck of his blue theatre pyjamas.

He walked up to the baby and touched his face gently, murmuring gently in Italian.

'For crying out loud, Nico, speak in English,' the anaesthetist complained cheerfully as he reached for a syringe. 'We're going to have communication problems here if you conduct this operation in Italian. The most I can do in your language is order a pizza.'

Nico laughed and his lean face was transformed from arrogant to devastatingly attractive. Suddenly Abby found herself thinking about the fact that they'd made a baby together.

Not in the traditional sense, of course, but still...

It was a strange thought that left her feeling hot inside and out.

She blushed slightly and at that moment he lifted his eyes and saw her. Their gazes locked and her breathing was suspended. An almost unbearable tension shimmered between them and she was unable to look away, unable to break the connection until finally he seemed to shake himself and turned back to the baby.

'If everything's all right here, I'll go and scrub.'

The anaesthetist nodded. 'Everything's fine.'

'Bene.'

With a last searing look at Abby Nico left the room, and she felt the tension drain out of her body.

The anaesthetist glanced up at her. 'Are you going into Theatre?'

Abby shook her head and smiled weakly. 'No.' *Her nerves couldn't stand it.* 'One of the other nurses from the ward is watching. I need to get back.'

The anaesthetist nodded as he concentrated on Thomas.

'Well, he's well and truly under, so you can go whenever you like.'

Abby made her way back to the ward and spent some time with Thomas's parents, who were beside themselves with worry. Then she busied herself on the ward, helping Heather with the drugs, feeding two of the babies who'd been in for investigation and changing a nasogastric tube.

Finally a call came through from Theatre, telling them that Thomas was off bypass and doing well.

Lorna stared at her, frantic with worry. 'What exactly does that mean—"off bypass"?'

'Thomas has had open heart surgery,' Abby reminded her, 'which means that in order to operate, they had to divert the blood flow away from his heart—basically a machine does the work of the heart for the duration of the operation.'

'So his heart stops?'

'Well, technically, yes. Once the surgeon has finished the operation, they start the heart again.'

Lorna rubbed a hand over her face and exchanged looks with her husband. 'So if he's off bypass, does that mean that Thomas is all right?'

'Well, it sounds positive, but we really have to wait to talk to Mr Santini to find out exactly how the operation went,' Abby said, knowing that it would be wrong of her to comment on the success of the operation without some knowledge of what had transpired in Theatre.

Lorna gave a wan smile. 'He's an amazing man. Fancy having the confidence to operate on a baby that small. My hands would be shaking too much.'

'I think I can guarantee that Mr Santini's hands don't shake,' Abby said lightly. In fact, she doubted whether Domenico Santini had ever had a single crisis of confidence in his life.

'He popped in to see us yesterday evening and again this

morning. He told us to call him Nico,' Lorna told her. 'He was really very informal and very kind.'

It was a shame he didn't seem to extend the same kindness to his personal life, Abby thought dully.

But all that mattered at the moment was that he did a good job on Thomas, she reminded herself firmly. Her personal problems could wait.

'His pressures are good.' Nico stared at the monitor and gave the anaesthetist a nod. 'How is he doing at your end?'

'He's doing all right but I'll be more relaxed once you're finished,' the anaesthetist said lightly.

'I'm going to close the chest.' Totally focused on the task in hand, Nico worked quickly, pausing occasionally to make an observation to his ever-increasing audience or ask a question of his assistant, Greg.

Finally, five hours after he'd started, he was finished. He stripped off his sterile gown and ran a hand over the back of his neck to relieve the tension.

His shoulders ached from standing in one position for so long and he walked through to the changing rooms, stripped off his clothes and stepped under the shower.

Then he grabbed a sandwich and a cup of coffee, knowing that by the time he'd finished Thomas would be settled in CICU.

He needed to check on Katherine Parker and speak to Thomas's parents.

Although there had been some complications that he hadn't anticipated, generally speaking he was pleased with the way the operation had gone.

Changing quickly, he checked his watch and strode down the corridor that linked the operating theatre to CICU.

The first person he saw was Abby and he stopped dead, his expert eye automatically running over the womanly curve of her hips and down her perfect legs. He frowned slightly. He hadn't ever thought of Abby as sexy until Carlo had mentioned it. In fact, he hadn't really given her any thought at all as a woman.

She was just someone who'd deceived him and given birth to his child.

Lowering his thick dark lashes, he surveyed her carefully, mentally stripping off the nurse's uniform and loosening her blonde hair from the childish ponytail.

The resulting image made him suck in his breath. There was no doubt in his mind that he'd been distracted by the events of the past few days or he would have noticed her sooner.

No red-blooded Italian male could miss those lush curves or the slight fullness of her lower lip.

As always in his judgement of women, Carlo was absolutely right.

Abby Harrington was gorgeous.

And after their encounter the previous night, Nico suspected that she was every bit as shy as he'd once thought.

He'd been totally aware of just how much effort and courage it had taken on her part to stand up to him and, despite his anger towards her, part of him was impressed. She'd defended her child like a tigress and he liked that about her.

She'd also clearly never expected him to find out that he was Rosa's father. Her shocked response to his announcement had been so genuine, so physical that despite his initial scepticism there was no way an experienced doctor like himself could dismiss it as feigned.

And it was now obvious to him that he was going to have a fight on his hands if he wanted the child.

And he did.

Nothing had prepared him for the raw emotion he'd felt when he'd held his child for the first time. The soft baby smell, her gurgle of delight when he'd held her close, her trusting acceptance of him had suddenly exposed a gaping hole in his life which he'd stubbornly refused to acknowledge before now.

Maybe Carlo was right. Maybe his reasons for wanting his daughter were more complicated than he'd claimed.

But as far as he was concerned, that didn't make any difference to the outcome.

He'd already contacted his lawyers and set the wheels in motion. One way or another he was going to make sure that he gained custody of Rosa.

Abby glanced up and her heart rate increased as she saw Nico approaching.

He'd obviously come straight from the shower and his dark hair was sleek and damp, his jaw dark with the beginnings of stubble.

He shot her a lingering glance and then checked the monitors, talked to the CICU nurse and the anaesthetist who ran the unit and then concentrated his attention on the parents.

She had to hand it to him, he was good with worried parents. He explained everything in simple language without being patronizing and by the time he left the unit Thomas's parents were looking much happier and had fallen over themselves to thank Nico.

'They need you back on the ward, Abby,' the sister on CICU called over to her, and Abby made her excuses, took a last look at little Thomas and made her way back to the ward.

'Sorry to call you back.' Heather was looking harassed and waved an arm towards the main part of the ward. 'We seem to be swamped all of a sudden and Mr Santini is going to do a teaching round, which, frankly, I need like a hole in the head. Would you mind feeding baby Hubbard? No one else can get her to take that bottle and you're a genius with babies. It's going to take ages because she gets breathless. When you've done that we've got a toddler from Paeds who needs admitting.'

At least feeding baby Hubbard would mean that she could hide away from Nico Santini, Abby thought, as she wandered through to the kitchen to collect the baby's feed.

She lifted the baby out of her cot and cuddled her close, talking gently to her as she coaxed her to take the bottle.

'There, sweetheart,' she crooned softly. 'I know this is a struggle for you so we'll take it slowly....'

Babies with heart problems often became breathless and had trouble feeding.

Once she'd encouraged the little one to take the teat, Abby settled down with a soft smile of satisfaction as the baby started to suck.

A noise in the doorway made her glance up and she stiffened as she saw Nico standing there.

'I gather they couldn't get her to take the bottle?' His dark eyes were concerned and he moved closer and squatted down next to her so that he could take a look at the baby.

'She's taking it now.' Abby flushed beneath the intensity of his gaze, uncomfortably aware of just how close he was. She had an enviable view of his sinfully long black lashes and just one move of her hand would have put her within touching distance of that glossy black hair. 'She gets very breathless so I suppose that doesn't help. She just needed a bit of persuasion.'

He nodded, those dark eyes thoughtful as they rested on her face. 'You are very good with her.'

The unexpected praise startled her and she looked up, flustered, as the door opened and the rest of the team of doctors and Heather entered the room.

Abby dropped her head and concentrated her attention on the baby, trying to work out what was happening. How could Nico behave as if nothing was wrong? As if they were just colleagues working side by side with no other interest? He'd made no reference to the night before, no mention of his plans for Rosa, and the anxiety was threatening to choke her.

'Thank goodness you've persuaded her to take that bottle,' Heather said, relief visible on her face. 'I might need you to sleep here if the night staff get stuck.'

Abby smiled, knowing that Heather wasn't serious. Everyone knew that she didn't work nights.

Once she'd finished feeding, Nico gently lifted the baby's fingers and examined them then uncoiled the stethoscope from his pocket.

Abby tried not to look at the dark hairs on his wrists or the way those skilled hands moved over the tiny baby. Having him so close unsettled her.

Finally he finished his examination and straightened. 'How is her weight?'

'She's losing weight,' Abby said flatly, watching as Heather handed him the chart. Nico's eyes flickered over it and he nodded and turned to Greg who was standing next to him, visibly tense in the presence of the consultant.

'Tell me about her.'

Greg cleared his throat. 'She's two days old and she was transferred from the postnatal ward late last night because one of the midwives thought she looked blue,' he said, shuffling through the notes to find what he wanted. 'The paediatrician suspects that she has congenital heart disease but he couldn't find a murmur and she has good pulses.'

Abby stared at the baby, noticing the blue tinge around her lips. 'Blue' or cyanotic babies didn't have enough oxygen in their blood.

Nico looked at him steadily. 'So what defects will I be considering in a cyanotic infant?'

Greg flushed slightly. 'Simple defects or complex defects—'

'Complex being?'

'Tetralogy of Fallot, transposition of the great arteries…' Greg continued to list them and Nico nodded approvingly.

'And what tests has she had?'

'She's had a chest X-ray and an echocardiogram,' Greg told him, flicking through the notes. 'Should we book her in for a cardiac catheterisation?'

Cardiac catheterisation meant passing a tiny tube into the baby's heart so that the doctor could get a close look at the defect and measure the pressures in the heart chambers, but Nico was shaking his head.

'Usually the diagnosis can be made with the echocardiogram and colour Doppler—we will see. If not then, yes, Jack can do a catheter.'

They talked for ages and Nico turned his attention to the other doctors, testing their knowledge and fielding their endless questions.

Abby had to hand it to him, he was good. There seemed to be no question he couldn't answer, discussing various options with the same supreme confidence with which he tackled everything in life.

Including taking her baby.

'This baby has transposition of the great arteries—TGA,' Nico said finally, after they'd reviewed all the tests together.

Greg stared at him. 'So she must have another defect or she'd be dead. TGA isn't compatible with life, is it? There is no communication between the systemic and the pulmonary circulation.'

'She has a PDA,' Nico said briefly, and Greg blinked.

'A patent ductus? But I didn't hear it when I listened to her chest.'

'But I did,' Nico said smoothly, folding his stethoscope and slipping it back inside his pocket, his eyes on the baby. 'She has a murmur that is characteristic of a patent ductus and that is why she is still alive. The blood vessel is connecting her aorta and pulmonary artery.'

'So what happens now?' Greg was looking distinctly uncomfortable that he hadn't detected the murmur and Abby almost felt sorry for him. He was a good doctor and everyone had to learn. Surely even Nico had been unsure early in his career?

She stole a glance at his glossy black hair, noting the arrogant tilt of his jaw and the sharp intelligence in his eyes.

Maybe not.

Nico Santini was super-bright and it was hard to imagine him ever having been unsure of anything.

'We give her Prostin and we check her oxygen saturation. If necessary, Jack can do a balloon atrial septostomy which will keep the blood mixing until we can do the repair,' Nico said immediately, taking a pen out of his pocket and writing something in the notes. 'We will do an arterial switch operation in the next couple of weeks. Where are the parents?'

'There's only the mother,' Abby told him quietly, supporting the little girl upright to help her breathing. 'This is her fourth child and the father left when he discovered she was pregnant again. She has very little help so she's had to go home to look after the other three. According to the postnatal ward she was distraught when the baby was kept in. She was expecting a six-hour discharge.'

'She is on her own? That is a dilemma,' Nico said quietly, a slightly frown touching his forehead. 'Are you sure she can't arrange child care so that she can be with the baby?'

'Not immediately.' Abby shook her head. 'She's doing her best to sort something out but for now she's just muddling along and visiting when she can.'

'I need to see her to explain the operation,' Nico said, and looked up at Greg. 'You are on call tonight—I want you to make yourself available to talk to her should she come in.'

Greg nodded. 'Of course. Will you be around if she wants to talk to you?'

Nico's dark eyes rested on Abby. 'I have plans for this evening,' he said evenly, 'but I will have my mobile with me. You can call me if it's urgent. Otherwise I will be in first thing tomorrow and I will be happy to speak to the mother then. This sort of news is always hard for parents to grasp. Speak slowly and clearly and check that they have understood you. Most people cannot even remember what a normal heart looks like so I find drawings helpful.'

He closed the notes and handed them to Greg then took a final look at the baby who was breathing rapidly and struggling to take the bottle from Abby.

'I will talk to Jack in the morning. If there is any change in her condition during the night, you can call me. Let's move on to the next patient.'

Heather rolled the notes trolley out of the room and Abby waited until the door clicked shut behind them then returned the baby to her cot with a sigh.

'I suppose you're lucky that he's going to operate on you,' she muttered, tucking the blankets around the dozing child. 'But somehow that doesn't make me feel much better. He might be a brilliant surgeon but he's very scary as a human being.'

What was she going to do?

How was she going to protect Rosa from him?

Nico was waiting for Abby when she came off duty, leaning casually against a low black sports car that shrieked of money.

'No limo?' Her voice was tart and she derived a certain satisfaction from the flash of surprise she saw in his dark eyes.

He obviously didn't expect her to talk back to him.

'I don't expect my chauffeur to wait around for me and

I was at the hospital last night,' he said smoothly, opening the door and jerking his head. 'Get in.'

Which meant that he did have a limo. And a chauffeur. *Ask a silly question…*

'I don't need a lift,' she said stiffly. 'I already have transport.'

And she wasn't ready to talk to him yet. She needed more time to work out her strategy. She also needed legal advice but she knew she couldn't afford that. Maybe she could persuade the bank to lend her some money.

'Transport?' He was frowning. 'You have a car?'

'Not exactly.' She avoided his gaze because looking at him affected her so dramatically. 'We take the bus.'

There was an ominous silence. 'You go home on a *bus*?'

'Well, two buses actually,' she told him, shifting Rosa more comfortably on her hip.

He was staring at her incredulously and it occurred to her that Nico Santini had probably never been on a bus in his life.

'I will give you a lift home.'

She clutched Rosa tightly, her reaction an instinctive rejection of his offer. 'I don't want a lift home. I'm fine on the bus.'

The skin over those incredible cheekbones was taut. '*Porca miseria*, my daughter is not travelling on a *bus*.'

If circumstances had been different she would have laughed at the look of horror on his face.

'It's a perfectly acceptable form of transport for most people,' Abby said defensively, and his eyes narrowed.

'But my daughter is not most people,' he said, his voice as smooth as silk. 'She will not travel on public transport—it is too risky.'

Abby blinked. Risky? For crying out loud, this was London in the rush-hour!

Then she remembered that Lucia had never been without a bodyguard at school.

To the Santinis it was a way of life.

'Look...' She kept her tone steady, more for her own benefit than his. She was trying to stay rational. 'No one knows Rosa is your daughter so she isn't at risk.'

'*I* know she's my daughter,' he pointed out immediately, 'and if I can get that information then so can others.'

Her heart gave a flutter and she stared at him. 'Are you seriously telling me that you think Rosa is at risk?'

'I don't want my daughter using public transport,' Nico said flatly. 'Now, get in the car. We have much to talk about.'

She shook her head. 'We have nothing to talk about. Nothing at all.'

He straightened with a fluid grace that reminded her of a lethal predator moving in for the kill. 'Then you should know that I have already contacted my lawyers and set in motion custody proceedings,' he said smoothly, and she felt her heart jump into her throat.

His lawyers?

'No judge is going to take a child away from a mother who loves her,' she said shakily, praying that she was right. She didn't have his ready access to endless funds so she had no way of obtaining her own legal advice. But surely the law wasn't that unfair?

Nico raised a dark eyebrow. 'You wish to discuss this in the hospital car park in front of an audience?'

Abby glanced around self-consciously and flushed as she intercepted several curious glances. 'I don't want to discuss it at all.'

Totally unperturbed, he gave a shrug and turned back to his car. 'In that case, I will see you in court.'

'No!' Her frantic protest made him stop and turn and he looked at her expectantly.

'You are ready to talk?'

She nodded, too upset to trust herself to speak. If she

opened her mouth she'd sob. And she'd rather swallow nails than lose control in front of Nico Santini again.

She clutched Rosa tighter and the little girl whimpered in protest.

'Let's go. She can go in the back,' Nico instructed, and she shook her head.

'I won't let her travel without a baby seat.'

Nico shot her a look of pure male exasperation. '*Dio*, you think I would be reckless with my own daughter? I purchased a seat today—take a look yourself if you don't believe me.'

Slight colour touching her cheeks, Abby peered into the back seat and saw the brand-new, top-of-the-range car seat strapped securely in the car. If she hadn't been in such a panic she would have laughed. She was willing to bet that he'd never put anything like that in his precious sports car before.

He drove fast but carefully, glancing into the back seat periodically to check on Rosa who was now fast asleep.

By the time they finally arrived at the tiny flat, Abby was shaking so much she wondered if her legs would hold her. Nico gathered the sleeping child against him and carried her into the house and laid her carefully on the sofa.

'Does she always sleep at this time?'

Abby bit her lip. 'Yes. It's the journey,' she muttered. 'It lulls her to sleep.'

His gaze was hard. 'In other words, she is tired from being left in a crèche all day.'

'She likes the crèche and I have to work!'

'Because you are a single parent,' he returned, his blue-black jaw tight and uncompromising.

'Plenty of people are single parents these days,' she said shakily, and he shot her a look of pure contempt.

'But rarely through choice. You made a conscious decision to have a baby without any financial or emotional support, and with that decision you chose to deprive her of all the things that a child has a right to. Most importantly, a father.'

Abby felt as though he'd stabbed her in the heart. It was true, of course. She *had* deprived Rosa of a father. But Rosa had a mother who adored her and that was worth a great deal.

Was Rosa really so badly off?

'I love her,' she choked, hanging onto her dignity by a thread. Never before in her life had she had to fight so hard not to cry. 'She's all I have in the world and if you take her…'

He frowned slightly, his dark eyes raking the pallor of her face. 'I no longer question your affection for her, but that doesn't alter the fact that she will have a better life with me.'

'How?' She gave up battling with tears and let them trickle down her face. So what if he thought she was a wimp? 'You're a complete workaholic, just like my father. When do you have time for a child? I can't see you giving up your job to look after her.'

'I have close family who would take on that responsibility,' he murmured, tension visible in his broad shoulders. 'Now that I'm convinced of your love for her, you will be allowed to see her.'

She scrubbed the tears away like a child and stared at him, appalled. 'And that's supposed to make it all right? I can see my own daughter *occasionally*?' He clearly believed that he was making an enormous concession and she gaped at him in disbelief. 'Why are you doing this? Why? If you want a child so badly, why not get married and have one of your own?'

There was a long silence and when he finally spoke his voice was flat, totally devoid of emotion. 'That isn't an option.'

'Getting married?' She stared at him stupidly, aware that

most of the members of her sex would have fallen over themselves to marry Nico Santini.

'Having more children.'

Abby was suddenly still, her attention caught by the tension in his shoulders. This had happened the last time she'd mentioned him having children of his own. 'But Rosa—'

'I developed testicular cancer almost two years ago.' He made the announcement with no emotion, in the same tone he might have used for reading the phone book. It was a statement of fact and no more. 'I had intensive chemotherapy. The cancer has gone but it is highly unlikely that I can father any more children.'

There was a shimmering silence while Abby digested that piece of information.

Nico Santini couldn't have more children?

With a stab of sympathy she reached out a hand and then let it drop to her side in sudden confusion. What was she thinking of? Her instinctive reaction had been to comfort him. Had she forgotten that he was the enemy? But, enemy or not, she felt sad for him.

She knew at first hand what it was like to be desperate for a family and suddenly it all fell into place.

'So that's why you want my child,' she whispered, and his dark gaze clashed with hers.

'She's my child, too. I tracked you down because I wanted to check that the child I fathered was happy and well cared for. Had Rosa been part of a loving family with two parents I never would have intervened, but in the circumstances I believe that she would be better off with me.'

Abby stared at him, her chest rising and falling as she breathed rapidly. 'I'm sorry that you can't have more children, I really am,' she croaked, her voice shaking with passion, 'but you can't take my Rosa. If you don't care about my feelings, at least think about her. I'm her mother. She needs me.'

'And she also needs her father.' His tone was devoid of

emotion. 'With me she will be part of a large and loving family who can give her everything.'

Abby's mouth was dry and the panic inside overwhelmed her. 'I'll get a lawyer.'

An ebony brow lifted. 'With what? Face it, there is no way you are in a position to contest my claim. One way or another, I will gain custody of Rosa.'

CHAPTER FOUR

'DON'T let anyone take her but me, will you?' Abby handed Rosa over to Karen who gave her a puzzled look.

'What on earth are you talking about? Who else is going to want to take her?'

Abby bit her lip. It was an impossible situation. She didn't want to tell Karen what was happening but she wanted to protect Rosa. How could she be sure that Nico wouldn't just take her?

'Just promise me,' she said urgently, scraping an escaped strand of blonde hair behind her ear.

'All right, I promise, but I think you've gone mad.' Karen gave Rosa a hug and smiled at Abby. 'How's Thomas Wood?'

'Doing all right yesterday,' Abby's eyes were still on her daughter. 'Might be back on the ward today. Depends how it goes.'

'So the guy was as good as his reputation, then.' Karen's tone was casual and Abby suppressed a sigh.

She didn't want to talk about Nico.

'He's a brilliant surgeon,' she said grudgingly, stooping to pick up her bag. 'I'm off now. Call me if you need me.'

She leaned forward to kiss Rosa and then forced herself to make her way to the ward, assuring herself that there was no way Karen would let the baby go with Nico Santini.

Heather was already on the ward and clearly harassed. 'They're having a JCC this morning. Do you want to attend? It would be a good learning experience for you.'

The JCC—the joint cardiac conference—was a meeting where everyone, including CICU staff, surgeons and cardiologist, got together to discuss each child and decide on the best plan of management.

'Are you sure you're not too busy to spare me?' Abby had mixed feelings. Part of her was interested in sitting in on the conference, but she knew that it would mean coming into close contact with Nico and she wasn't sure that she could handle that.

'No, but I want you to go,' Heather said generously. 'They're transferring Thomas Wood back from CICU later on this morning so as long as you're back for that, we should manage fine. Do you know what happens at one of those meetings?'

'Not really.' Abby shook her head briefly. 'I always assumed everyone just pooled information and discussed the best way forward.'

'Well, that's right. Basically they discuss each child,' Heather explained. 'They look at the catheter and the echo and decide what type of operation is needed and how quickly. Whether it's an emergency that needs to be done in the next twenty-four hours or whether it should be delayed for a couple of months. If it's an emergency, they have to arrange a theatre slot and check that there are beds in CICU. I think you should go.'

'All right, if you're sure.' Abby made her way along to the meeting room and slipped into a seat towards the back of the room.

Nico and Jack, the cardiologist, were already deep in conversation about baby Hubbard.

'I've scheduled her for balloon atrial septostomy this afternoon,' Jack was saying, and Nico nodded approval.

'So we can discontinue the prostaglandin. Good.'

Andrea, the cardiac case manager who was the link between the ward, doctors and parents, made a few notes on her pad. 'So she can go home while she waits for her op?'

Nico frowned and turned his gaze to Abby. 'You said

that she has three other children and is on her own. Can she manage the baby, do you think?'

Everyone in the room suddenly seemed to be looking at her, and Abby felt her face grow hot. 'I'll talk to her when she visits tonight.'

After their emotionally charged confrontation the night before, how could he be so relaxed?

'Let us know the outcome.' Nico gave a brief nod and Andrea glanced between him and Jack.

'So if the mother is happy, when will you send her home?'

'Jack needs to do the atrial septostomy and then we will monitor her oxygen saturation,' Nico told her. 'If she maintains it between 60 and 70 per cent, we will send her home. If not, then she stays in and we operate.'

'And if her sats are all right, when will you operate?'

Jack looked at Nico. 'Two weeks?'

Nico nodded and they reviewed the tests together and discussed the operation.

When they were satisfied with the plan of action they moved on to the next child.

By the end of the meeting Abby's head was reeling. Each child had been reviewed in detail, with everyone in the room contributing to the discussion.

Back on the ward the CICU nurse handed over Thomas Wood and briefed Abby in detail.

'He's doing well. We've taken out the chest drain and the catheter. We're restricting his fluid intake because we don't want to overload the heart so we've been keeping him fairly dry, but for the next twenty-four hours he can have 65 mls of fluid per kilo.'

Which meant calculating everything, including feed and drugs.

The nurse finished the handover and Abby glanced at the monitors, checking that the baby's oxygen saturation was satisfactory. Then she used the dinamap to check Thomas's blood pressure.

'Do you really need to check his chest?' Lorna was looking pale and exhausted. 'I hate seeing the scar on his little body.'

'It's hard, I know, but we're giving him drugs for the pain and you'll be amazed by how quickly it heals,' Abby told her, her voice sympathetic. 'I have to check it for signs of bleeding, but it will only take a second.'

Very carefully she lifted the dressing and checked the stenotomy wound, satisfying herself that all looked well.

As she was replacing the dressing Nico strolled into the room, followed by a team of more junior doctors.

'Lorna…' he put a lean brown hand on her shoulder '…how are you feeling?'

'I'm doing fine.' Lorna gave him a shaky smile and her eyes filled. 'I don't know how to thank you.'

'No thanks are necessary.' Nico walked towards the cot and checked the stenotomy wound himself. Then his eyes lifted to the monitors, checking the readings. 'That is all looking good. The operation went well.'

Lorna breathed out heavily. 'When do you think he might be able to go home?'

Nico smiled. 'Perhaps in another week. We will need to keep an eye on him and see how he goes.'

He took time to answer all Lorna's questions and when he finally left the room Abby stared after him helplessly, wondering how on earth she was going to fight him.

It was towards the end of her shift when the hospital crèche called to say that Rosa had developed a temperature.

Abby felt her heart lurch. She'd known that Rosa was slightly off colour but she'd been hoping that it was nothing more than a teething problem. Now it seemed as though it could be something more.

Feeling guilty for deserting the ward when they were

busy, she asked Heather's permission to finish early and then she made her way down to the crèche.

Rosa was crying miserably, her cheeks pink and blotched with tears.

'Oh, sweetheart…' Abby reached out for her and cuddled her close, feeling just how hot she was.

'I gave her some Calpol half an hour ago,' Karen told her, 'but so far it hasn't had any effect. You were obviously right about her coming down with something. Mother's instinct, I suppose.'

'Maybe. Thanks, Karen.' Still trying to soothe a wailing Rosa, Abby gathered up her bags and struggled down the corridor. There was no way she could take the child on a bus like this. She'd have to blow the last of her month's pay cheque and take a taxi home.

As she reached the hospital entrance Rosa's wails increased and Abby felt more and more anxious.

Was it something serious or was it just a simple virus?

One of the most frightening things about being a single parent was handling a sick child alone.

'How is Rosa doing?' Nico's smooth tones came from right behind her and she turned in dismay.

Typical.

He was just about the last person that she wanted to bump into at this precise moment. He'd probably find some way of blaming her for Rosa's illness and use it against her.

'She's not well and I need a taxi.'

'I know she isn't well,' he said calmly. 'I was standing next to Heather when you asked if you could leave, but you were in such a state that you didn't even notice me. And you don't need to call a taxi. I'll take you home.'

She started to shake her head and then realised how foolish that was. She needed to get Rosa home as fast as possible, and as there was no sign of a taxi Nico was the only option.

'All right.' She tried not to sound grudging. 'But I want to call at the surgery on the way home so that our GP can check her over.'

Nico unlocked the car and held the door open for her. 'Abby, I'm a doctor, remember? I'll check her over myself when we get her home.'

Abby gritted her teeth. 'You're a heart surgeon.'

'Well, believe it or not, I am vaguely familiar with other parts of the anatomy,' he said dryly, and she bit her lip.

'I just don't think you're the right person.'

She didn't want him near Rosa. She didn't trust him.

He was totally unmoved by her declaration. 'Just get in the car.'

She looked at him in helpless frustration. The man just didn't understand the word 'no'!

But she needed to get Rosa home.

'You must have been an awful toddler,' she muttered as she strapped Rosa carefully into the car seat.

One dark eyebrow rose. 'You wish to know about my childhood?'

'No.' She closed the passenger door and stalked round to the driver's side. 'I don't want to know anything about you. Frankly, I wouldn't care if I never saw you again.'

'Oh, you're going to see me again, Abby,' he said softly. 'You're going to see plenty of me, but now isn't the time to talk about that. Now, get in and let's get her home.'

Once inside, Nico immediately examined Rosa.

'I can't see anything obvious wrong with her.' Finally he put down his stethoscope and looked at the baby thoughtfully. 'Her chest is clear, her throat is slightly pink but nothing dramatic and her ears are fine. We'll just watch her for a few hours and see how she goes.'

'*We*?'

Every nerve in her body frayed with worry, Abby stared at him blankly. 'Does that mean that you're planning to stay here?'

'*Sì.*' His black eyes clashed with hers. 'I won't leave her while she is ill and it will give us a chance to talk further.'

'Oh, yippee,' Abby muttered, and his eyes narrowed.

'I haven't eaten yet. I'm very hungry.'

'You know where the kitchen is,' Abby said tartly. 'Help yourself to anything you find.'

If he was expecting her to cook for him, he could think again.

For a brief moment she thought she saw surprise in his dark eyes. Well, tough, she thought, cuddling Rosa on her lap. Doubtless he was used to women falling over themselves to service his every need. She had no intention of joining them.

'You should get something to eat yourself.'

'I'm not hungry.' Distracted, she put her hand on Rosa's chest to check her temperature again. 'She's so hot....'

Nico's phone rang and as he entered into a detailed discussion with one of the doctors at the hospital, he strode out of the room and closed the door quietly behind him. Abby kicked off her shoes and curled up more comfortably in the old rocking chair that she'd found in a junk shop and lovingly restored. She knew that she ought to have followed him and asked him about his intentions but she was too much of a coward. And, anyway, Rosa needed her. The toddler was clinging to her like a limpet and there was no way she was letting her go.

About twenty minutes later something about the way Rosa was breathing made her suddenly anxious.

Reaching out a hand, she touched the baby's chest again and felt a dart of panic as she realised how hot she was.

'Oh, sweetheart, you're burning up again.' She checked her watch but it was too soon to give her any more medicine.

Rosa barely reacted to her touch, lying listlessly on her lap, showing no interest in anything. Really worried, Abby stood up and put the little girl in her cot, thinking that cuddling her so close must be raising her temperature. She was too hot and needed to be cooled down fast.

Rosa protested feebly as Abby put her down but within seconds of being placed in the cot the little girl went rigid and started to fit. Abby felt panic slam through her body.

'Nico!'

Frantic with worry, she shouted his name, anxiety about Rosa overriding all other considerations. Whatever else he might be, she knew he was a superb doctor.

He was beside her in an instant.

'What's the matter?'

'She got hotter and hotter and now she's fitting.' Abby felt sick and watched helplessly while Nico swiftly cleared the child's airway and adjusted her position.

'Call an ambulance,' he instructed calmly. 'If she doesn't stop fitting she'll need diazepam and I don't have any with me.'

Her whole body trembling, Abby sprinted along to the sitting room and dialled with a shaking hand.

By the time she returned to the bedroom Rosa had stopped fitting but her lips were blue and she didn't respond as Nico swiftly stripped her of the rest of her clothes.

'We need to bring her temperature down. Do you have a fan?'

Abby shook her head, gulping in air as she stared at her limp daughter. 'No.'

'Well, let's start by opening the window.' Nico dropped the clothes on the floor and left just the nappy on. 'We'll cover her in just a cotton sheet. What time did she have paracetamol?'

'Just two hours ago,' Abby told him, feeling utterly helpless as she looked at her daughter. 'She can't have any more yet.'

'But we can give her ibuprofen when she gets to hospital. She's still too drowsy to take it from us anyway. Her pulse is a bit fast and so is her breathing but she seems OK.'

Nico was checking the child's ears and throat again. 'Her pharynx is still slightly red. But that is all I can find wrong with her. Her temperature is very high, so I'm sure this is a febrile seizure and nothing more than that.'

Abby stared at him, desperately hoping that he was right. She was well aware that young children with very high temperatures could fit, but she was also aware that some of those went on to have epilepsy.

Nico looked at her and frowned. 'It is not epilepsy,' he said shortly, clearly reading her mind. 'I am as sure as I can be of that. She is the right age for a febrile seizure and her temperature is impossibly high.'

Abby voiced the other fear that had been nagging at her. 'Could she have meningitis?'

He hesitated. 'It's possible,' he said finally, 'but I think it unlikely. However, they might well want to do a lumbar puncture to be sure.'

At that moment Abby heard the ambulance arrive and ran to the door to let them in.

Nico spoke to them and within minutes Rosa was loaded into the ambulance.

Abby hesitated by the doors of the ambulance. 'Will you follow us?'

A glimmer of surprise showed in his dark eyes before he masked the reaction and nodded. 'Of course. I'll be right behind you.' He hesitated for a moment and then put a hand on her shoulder. 'Try not to worry. I'm sure it is just a virus that will settle in time. You know that it is common for children of this age to fit. They are not always able to control their temperatures like adults. It doesn't mean that she'll have long-term problems.'

She nodded, her lower lip caught between her teeth. She felt as though she was going crazy. She knew she ought to hate him and yet she was hugely relieved that he'd been there to deal with Rosa. For once she was grateful that he was a control freak. She'd needed someone to take over.

Once at the hospital, Nico didn't leave Rosa's side.

'We need to do a lumbar puncture,' the paediatrician said, and the colour drained from Abby's face.

'You think she has meningitis?'

Nico frowned at her. 'It's a routine check—they are trying to find the source of the infection. She has a high temperature and she's had a fit. We must check for meningitis. Go and get a coffee.'

Abby shook her head, knowing that someone had to hold the child while the doctor performed the test.

'No,' she said shakily. 'I'll do it. I want to be there for her. I'm her mother.'

Nico took her to one side so that no one could hear her. 'You're also so stressed that you will be doing her no favours,' he said quietly. 'Don't be stubborn. You are in no fit state to hold the child. I will do it.'

Abby pulled away from him, shaking her head. 'No. She needs her mother.' She walked quickly back to the paediatrician who was preparing for the test.

In the end it wasn't as bad as she'd feared. Rosa was so poorly that she barely flinched when the doctor put the needle in her back to draw off some of the spinal fluid.

'It's clear,' he said as he let the fluid drop into the bottle. 'It looks fine but I'll get this off to the lab. I suspect that this is just a virus that we won't be able to identify. We'll keep her in and see how she goes. One of you is welcome to stay with her.'

The paediatric ward was well designed, with beds next to the cots so that a parent could stay with the child.

Embarrassed that the paediatrician had assumed that they were in some way connected, Abby waited for Nico to correct him but he didn't.

Instead he questioned the other doctor minutely, checking that all the necessary tests had been performed and that every possibility had been covered.

For once Abby was thoroughly relieved that he was there.

'We've given her more Calpol and ibuprofen so we'll just keep an eye on her temperature and see what happens,' the paediatrician said, peeling off his sterile gloves and tossing them in the bin. 'I think you'll find that she settles during the night.'

He left the room and Nico turned to Abby.

'You aren't prepared for a stay in hospital. Do you need me to go home and fetch you something?'

She blushed. It sounded ridiculously intimate, and yet only a few hours earlier this man had been voicing his intention to take her child away from her.

'I don't need anything,' she muttered, all her attention focused on Rosa who was breathing noisily in the cot.

'In that case, I'm going to pop back down to the ward,' he told her. 'I want to check on a couple of patients so I'll see you later.' He hesitated briefly and then looked at her, his gaze disturbingly direct. 'You were brave to hold her for that lumbar puncture when you were so upset.'

Without waiting for a reply, he left the room and Abby stared after him, trying to work out the implications of what he'd just said. Was he praising her? Was he finally acknowledging that Rosa needed her?

And if that was the case, surely he would see that it wouldn't be fair to take Rosa away?

Rosa awoke at three in the morning, fretful and crying for her mother. A nurse was standing over her, checking her temperature.

'Is it OK to hold her?' Abby struggled to sit up and looked at the nurse anxiously in the dim light. 'I don't want to send her temperature skyward again. I know she needs to be kept cool.'

The nurse smiled softly as she checked the thermometer. 'Don't worry about that. Her temperature has come down a lot and I think what she really needs is a cuddle with her mother.'

As Rosa snuggled contentedly into her chest, Abby looked up and saw Nico standing in the doorway.

His dark eyes were watchful, his expression impossible to read as he studied the two of them.

'I-is something the matter?' Abby stammered slightly, and held Rosa closer. 'Do you think I should put her back in the cot?'

Whatever she felt about him as a man, she respected his opinion as a doctor.

'No, the nurse is right.' His voice was gruff. 'She needs her mother.'

For a tense moment their eyes met and Abby knew that they were both thinking the same thing—*that if he carried out his threat, he was going to be taking Rosa from her mother for ever.*

Vulnerable from lack of sleep and worry, Abby felt her eyes fill.

'Nico—'

'Not now.' His voice was low and gruff. 'We'll talk about it later.'

So he knew exactly what she was thinking.

Seeing her tears and misinterpreting the cause, the nurse slipped an arm around her shoulder.

'There, pet, don't upset yourself. She's going to be fine.'

Abby struggled to pull herself together but when she finally looked up there was no sign of Nico.

He reappeared the following morning, his expression grim. 'We have a new problem, which I'm afraid I didn't anticipate.'

Abby looked up from sponging Rosa. 'What's wrong?'

'I underestimated my importance to the British tabloid

press.' His tone bitter, he flung several newspapers down on the bed next to her.

She blanched as she saw the photo and read the story.

ITALIAN BILLIONAIRE IN PATERNITY CLAIM

Sources have revealed that top heart surgeon Domenico Santini, heir to the Santini fortune, has recently discovered that he is the father of a baby daughter. Nurse Abigail Harrington is known to be close friends with Santini's sister and has never revealed the identity of the father of her child. However, friends confirm that she was in Italy two years ago and there is speculation that the pair might have had a relationship. Santini has refused to comment on the rumours, but a spokesman for the hospital has confirmed that he will be working there for the foreseeable future.

Abby dropped the paper and stared at him, appalled. 'Where did they get this information?'

'That isn't important. What is important now is protecting Rosa.'

She looked at him blankly. 'Wh-what do you mean?' Why would Rosa need protection?

He muttered under his breath in Italian and raked long fingers through his glossy dark hair. 'I can't believe that you are that naïve. The press are now camped outside the hospital entrance,' he said through gritted teeth, his eyes midnight black with anger. 'Given the opportunity, they will slip past Security and find their way up here.'

'But why are they so interested?'

'Because my sex life has always interested the media,' he said bitterly. 'I forgot just how bad your press is over here.'

Abby stared at the paper again and her cheeks flushed. 'They think we've had a relationship....'

He gave a short laugh. 'And maybe we should be thankful for that.'

Abby looked up at him, knowing that he was right. If the press ever found out the truth, they would have a field day.

'Could they find out?' she whispered, and his jaw tightened.

'I don't know. I suppose it is possible,' he said finally, lines of strain showing around his handsome features. 'We need to be prepared for that.'

As he finished speaking a burly man appeared in the doorway and spoke to Nico in Italian.

Nico replied and then looked at Abby. 'This is Matteo Parini. He is on my father's security team. He will stay with you until Rosa is allowed out of hospital. You'll both be safe with him.'

Security team?

Abby's jaw dropped. He'd arranged for her to have a *bodyguard*? Just what exactly was he afraid of?

'S-surely we're s-safe enough in here,' she stammered, but Nico ignored her, speaking to the other man in rapid Italian and then turning back to her, his expression cold and unsmiling.

'I have a ward round in ten minutes and then a theatre list. I'll try and pop up at lunchtime. In the meantime, don't leave the ward and if you need anything at all, ask Matt. He'll arrange it for you.'

With that he turned on his heel and left her staring after him with a stunned expression on her face.

Matt gave her a sympathetic smile. 'He has a tendency to dominate but take it from me—he has your best interests at heart.'

Which confirmed that Matt didn't have the slightest clue what was going on, she thought dully. Of course Nico didn't have her interests at heart. He had his own interests at heart, which was why he was protecting Rosa.

'I don't understand any of this—' She broke off, and

looked at him doubtfully. 'Are you going to spend the whole day here?'

Matt nodded. 'There are a herd of journalists outside the hospital and now the story is out, goodness knows who else might be lurking.'

Lurking? Her heart missed a beat. 'Are you talking about kidnap?'

Matt gave her a reassuring smile. 'It's only a precaution.' He glanced into the cot and his hard expression softened. 'She's the spitting image of her father.'

Which meant that there was no point in denying her paternity, Abby thought helplessly. Why couldn't Rosa have looked more like her?

'How did they find out about Rosa?'

Matt let out a long breath. 'We don't know that yet, but you can be sure that Nico will find out and I certainly wouldn't want to be in the culprit's shoes when he does. He's not a man to cross.'

He looked up as a cleaner tapped on the door.

'Can I come in and do the room?'

Matt straightened and his shoulders virtually filled the doorway. 'Sorry, no. Only medical staff.'

The cleaner scowled. 'I've got a job to do.'

'And so have I,' Matt replied calmly. 'If there's a problem I'll clear it with your supervisor.'

His tone was civil but the cleaner looked him in the eye and clearly saw something that made her back away.

Matt watched her go and then relaxed against the doorframe again.

'Why wouldn't you let her in?' Abby asked hesitantly, totally out of her depth. 'She was just a cleaner.'

'Was she?' Matt gave her a gentle smile. 'You really are an innocent, aren't you? She could be press. Or someone else. No one comes in this room that isn't essential. Nico's orders, I'm afraid.'

'I don't understand any of this. How did you get here so quickly? The papers only came out this morning.'

'They were printed last night,' Matt explained patiently, 'and we had warning that the story was going to break yesterday. And I was already here.'

'Already here? You mean Nico has a bodyguard in England?'

Matt gave a rueful smile. 'Not exactly, although strictly speaking he ought to. He always says that he can't operate with me hanging over his shoulder. And the honest truth is he can handle himself as well as I can. He's an expert in martial arts and he can use a gun with a precision that makes me green with envy. But basically the guy just wants to be a doctor and he can't stand the fuss that goes with being a Santini.'

'So why were you already in England?'

'It was a compromise. The boss wanted me close by in case anything happened, and as it turns out he was right.'

'The boss?'

'Nico's father. He owns and runs Santini Medical Supplies.' Matt looked at her curiously. 'You really don't know any of this, do you?'

No, but she'd heard of Santini Medical Supplies. Who hadn't? They were one of the biggest medical equipment companies in the world.

Abby realised that if Matt had read the papers, he probably thought that she and Nico had been involved in some sort of steamy relationship in the past, which meant that she should have known all these details about him.

At that moment Rosa woke up and Abby lifted her out of her cot and gave her a cuddle, relieved to find that she was much cooler.

The rest of the morning past quickly and the doctors came back to look at Rosa just before lunchtime.

'She seems much better.' The paediatrician nodded with satisfaction as he finished examining her. 'You can take her home this afternoon if you're happy with that. If you were on your own with her I'd suggest you stayed another night just for your peace of mind, but as her father is a doctor I'm sure you'll be fine at home.'

'Oh, but—' Abby started to correct him but Nico's voice interrupted her.

'That will be fine,' he said smoothly. 'I've arranged it so that I'm not on call tonight. I will be able to watch her.'

'Fine.' The paediatrician nodded, went through the test results with Nico and then made for the door. 'Oh, by the way…' He gave a rueful smile. 'You've attracted quite a lot of attention outside. If you need any help making your exit, I can call hospital security.'

Matt glanced at Nico who shook his head briefly. 'I have my own staff who are well used to dealing with this sort of thing, but thank you for your help.'

The doctor left and Abby glanced at Nico, wondering what he had planned. He was speaking to Matt in rapid Italian and the other man nodded and left the room at a brisk walk. Nico turned to Abby, his expression calm.

'Gather her things together and we'll take her home.'

Abby didn't even question how he planned to achieve a discreet exit with half the British press camped outside the hospital entrance. He clearly had it all covered.

As soon as she'd stuffed the last of her possessions into her bag, Nico took her arm and led her into the corridor and into the lift. They went down to the basement and emerged into one of the underground corridors which mapped their way beneath the hospital.

Matt was waiting, a mobile phone in his hand and a look of anticipation on his face.

Abby felt her heart lurch. They were obviously expecting trouble.

Together they flanked her as they walked briskly up the corridor, taking various turns that left her completely confused.

'I have no idea where we are,' she confessed to Matt at one point, 'and I work in this hospital. How do you know where to go?'

'It's my job,' he answered lightly, taking her arm and steering her into a small corridor.

He spoke in a low tone and for the first time Abby noticed the tiny earpiece. She glanced at Nico.

'It's like being with James Bond,' she muttered, and he gave a wry smile.

'The technology my father uses is probably more advanced.' He put a hand on her arm and looked questioningly at Matt who gave a brief nod.

'You follow Matt,' Nico instructed. 'I will take Rosa.'

Without arguing she did as he ordered, handing over her daughter and staying close to the bodyguard. He led her up a narrow flight of steps and she emerged into the daylight to find a limousine waiting.

She stopped dead but Nico gave her a sharp push from behind and she stumbled into the car without further question, aware that it had pulled away from the kerb before the door had even closed behind them.

Nico strapped Rosa into a child seat and spoke quickly to the driver.

Abby glanced over her shoulder but there was no sign of anyone following them.

'Where is this entrance?' She worked in the hospital and didn't recognise it at all.

'It's the psychiatric unit,' Matt told her. 'We arranged for a blonde woman to walk out of the paediatric entrance with a dark-haired toddler to keep the press busy. They should have realised by now that it wasn't us, but hopefully it will have distracted them sufficiently for us to get away.'

Abby blinked. It was a completely different world.

Rosa started to fret slightly and Abby slid across the seat and gave her a kiss.

'It's OK, sweetheart,' she murmured gently, 'we'll soon be home.'

She glanced out of the window to see where they were and realised that they weren't anywhere near her flat. They were driving away from the East End, through the centre of London and past the Serpentine.

'Where are we going?'

'Somewhere safe.' Nico leaned back against the seat and exchanged a glance with Matt.

She looked at him anxiously. 'But—'

'We'll discuss it later.'

Obviously he didn't want to talk about it in front of Matt and his driver, and she slunk closer to Rosa, feeling horribly out of her depth.

This couldn't be happening to her. She led a totally normal life, boring by some standards, but that was the way she liked it. She liked the predictability, the security of her existence. Since Nico Santini had strode into her life, all that had been turned upside down.

They drove for about twenty minutes and then the car plunged into an underground car park and came to a halt by a bank of lifts.

Matt was out of the car in a second, holding the door open for Abby. Nico took Rosa and they stepped into the lift.

It purred up to the top of the building and when the doors opened Abby gave a gasp of surprise.

A glass atrium spilled light onto a marble hallway complete with a fountain which gushed water over carefully placed rocks.

Rosa squealed with delight and reached out both hands.

Nico smiled indulgently. Understanding what she wanted, he immediately walked his daughter over to the fountain and let her hold her hand under the water, his smile broadening as she splashed him with a delicious giggle.

Matt grinned at his employer. 'Nice to know that someone likes it, boss.'

Nico gave a wry smile and turned to look at Abby. 'When this apartment was built, the designer was given free rein,' he explained. 'We all thought she'd gone overboard with the fountain. Maybe we were wrong.'

'Rosa loves water.' Abby was watching him in amazed fascination. He was so visibly smitten with his daughter. She tried to imagine another human being splashing him with water and being rewarded with a smile, and failed dismally. If she'd had any doubts about his feelings for his daughter, they vanished in an instant. 'If this is your apartment, surely the press know about it?'

'Not yet.' Nico shifted Rosa in his arms and walked towards a large living room. 'We've used various means of keeping it a secret, but I have no doubt that it will take them very little time to find us.'

Abby looked at him in dismay. 'And then what happens?'

'Even if they locate the building, this apartment is totally secure.' Nico turned to the other two men and spoke in Italian. They both swiftly melted into the background, leaving Abby and Nico alone.

'I apologise for bringing you here with no warning, but I didn't want to discuss our situation in front of my staff.'

Well, of course he didn't. Threatening to take her daughter hardly did him credit, did it?

'Why didn't you just drop us at home?'

His mouth tightened. 'Your flat would not have been safe.'

'But if they find out that we're together here, it just confirms the rumours.'

'I think we need to accept that this is one story that is going to be impossible to deny.' His gaze was steady. 'Unfortunately they are already convinced that Rosa is my daughter, and one only has to look at her to see the resemblance. Also, you have always concealed the identity of her father from everyone. Such secrecy will inevitably fuel the speculation that she is my daughter.'

Colour flooded her cheeks and she sank into the nearest chair with a thump.

'So...' She worked hard to keep the tremor out of her voice. 'We need to decide what we're going to do.'

'I've already decided.' Nico turned towards her, broad-shouldered and handsome, arrogantly sure of himself and totally in control. 'We will get married as soon as it can be arranged.'

CHAPTER FIVE

ABBY stared at him stupidly.

'Married?' Her voice was little more than a squeak. 'You have to be joking.'

'If you knew me better, you would know that I never joke about anything as serious as marriage,' Nico drawled, his eyes holding a hint of humour. 'Come through to the kitchen. You haven't eaten anything since yesterday lunch-time and we need to see if we can tempt Rosa with some food.'

Food?

'But—'

'Abby…' He dragged long fingers through his black hair, his voice weary and heavily accented. 'I have been up all night and I had a long theatre list this morning. Then I had to dodge the press in order to return to my home. I'm not exactly at my best. We'll sort out Rosa and discuss the details later.'

Details?

Her slim fingers dug into damp palms. 'You're the last man in the world I'd want to marry. I don't want to marry you and you can't possibly want to marry me.' She blurted the words out impulsively and then clamped her teeth on her lip and braced herself for the full force of his anger.

Instead he smiled, clearly amused by her passionate declaration. 'Actually, I'm becoming more taken with the idea by the minute. You're the first woman I've ever met who doesn't have designs on me. In fact, you don't seem to want a single thing from me, and I find that completely novel.'

Abby stared at him in mystified fascination. He just

didn't get it, did he? She'd just refused him but he hadn't even heard her.

He truly didn't understand the meaning of the word 'no'.

Maybe she needed to be blunt. 'You barged into my life without warning and threatened to take my child from me. You have the sensitivity of a sledgehammer. Give me one reason why I would even consider marrying you.'

'Well, most women start with my wallet,' he drawled softly, and she gave an incredulous laugh.

In her opinion, all the money in the world wouldn't compensate for being in a loveless marriage. 'I'm not interested in your money. Money doesn't make a family happy,' she said, working hard to hang onto her composure. 'It's love and attention from parents that does that.'

Something that she'd never had.

'I agree,' he said confidently, his dark eyes fixed on her face. 'And Rosa will have that. You cannot possibly be pretending that she won't benefit from also living with her father.'

She could barely hide her frustration. 'But we don't love each other.'

He frowned impatiently. 'I admire you professionally and I appreciate your deep love for Rosa. The rest is irrelevant. Marriages based on love frequently come unstuck. Mutual understanding is all we need. I don't need you to love me.'

He admired her professionally? He appreciated her love for Rosa? He certainly didn't win any awards for romantic proposals of marriage.

She looked at him helplessly. 'And if I say no?'

'Then you lose Rosa.'

His flat statement made the colour drain out of her face and she forced herself to face the facts.

For all his faults, Nico had struck up a warm relationship with his daughter in the short time they'd known each other. Seeing them together just sharpened the guilt she felt at depriving Rosa of the chance to grow up with a father.

Marrying Nico Santini would undoubtedly benefit Rosa, but what about the price for her personally?

Every time he walked into a room her stomach tied itself in knots and her body shook with nervous tension. How could she contemplate marrying him?

'There must be another way,' she said helplessly, and he shrugged.

'There isn't,' he said calmly, walking towards the kitchen without a backward glance.

She followed him almost at a run, outrage mingling with panic.

He settled Rosa in a high chair and started opening cupboards. 'What does she eat?'

'Anything. Everything.' Abby felt as though her head was bursting. He seemed to think that the conversation was finished. 'She isn't fussy.'

'*Bene.* She can have pasta.' Nico removed a packet from the cupboard.

'But you can't possibly—' She broke off in mid-sentence, suddenly distracted by the fact that he was reading the back of the packet. 'What are you doing?'

'Reading the instructions.'

'Instructions?' She looked at him incredulously. 'It's just dried pasta. You cook it in boiling water. What do you normally do with it?'

'Normally I have a chef,' he announced, emptying the contents into a large saucepan. 'But I wanted to have privacy while we sort out details so he has gone with Matt and my driver.'

Chef?

'You're cooking too much,' she said automatically as she saw the volume of pasta he'd poured into the pan. 'That's enough to feed an army.'

She got to her feet and walked across to him, taking matters into her own hands.

'I can't believe that you can do a complex heart operation but you can't cook pasta.' She poured half the pasta back into the packet and flicked the switch on the kettle.

'Abby,' his voice was patient. 'I spend eighteen hours a day at the hospital, sometimes more. I certainly don't want to return home and start cooking a meal. Fortunately, I don't have to. If you open the fridge you'll find a variety of sauces that my chef prepared earlier. Help yourself to whatever you think she'd like.'

Abby found a Bolognese sauce and emptied it into a pan.

Nico looked over her shoulder. 'Will she need that puréed? There's a gadget somewhere in the kitchen…'

'She's a year old,' Abby reminded him, giving him an odd look. 'She eats everything that you and I eat in exactly the same format.'

He lifted his eyebrows. 'She doesn't mind lumps?'

'She loves lumps. Toast, roast potatoes—you name it, she eats it.' Abby glanced at him and took a deep breath. 'How do you plan to be a good father when you can't even cook for her and you don't know what she eats?'

'I'm learning as fast as I can, but I came to that same conclusion myself,' he confessed calmly, watching as she stirred the source. 'Last night when I saw you with her in the hospital I realised that Rosa is very attached to you.'

Her heart lifted. 'But if you can see that, surely you can't threaten to take her from me.'

'I also believe that she needs her father.' His tone was cool. 'Which is why we will get married. It is the perfect solution.'

He really was serious.

Abby's whole body felt hot and strange. The mere thought of being married to Nico Santini made her shake with nerves. On the other hand, he just meant it as a business arrangement, she assured herself. He certainly didn't have any feelings for her personally. He wasn't suggesting that they become intimate.

Even so, the whole idea was ridiculous. He was a billionaire from one of the oldest and wealthiest families in Italy, whereas she…

The irony of the situation wasn't lost on her and she almost laughed aloud. There were probably thousands of women out there who would have done anything to be in her position.

'You can't possibly marry a penniless nurse,' she muttered, concentrating all her attention on the sauce as she attempted to reason with him. 'Your family would have a fit.'

'The opinion of my family is totally irrelevant, but I can assure you that my mother would be totally indifferent to your financial situation. She doesn't care about things like that. She would just be delighted to see me married,' he said wryly. 'Especially as you are the mother of my child.'

'But I'm *not*. I mean, not in *that* way. I mean we never—But if you marry me they'll think we did…' She broke off, painfully embarrassed. She'd never had this sort of conversation with anyone in her life before. 'They'll think we—'

'Were lovers?' Nico's tone was blunt. 'And that's exactly what we want them to think, *angelo*. The truth would undoubtedly sell more papers but I, for one, would rather not have the details of Rosa's paternity splashed across the press for all to read.' He shrugged off his jacket and removed his tie. 'If you marry me, we will be able to tell people that we had a relationship when you were on holiday in Italy, that I was unaware that you had become pregnant until recently. We are now reunited and deeply in love.'

Deeply in love?

Abby gaped at him. 'But why would you say that?'

'To please my mother and keep the press happy,' he said calmly, undoing his top button with lean, brown fingers.

'And because I don't want a breath of gossip attached to Rosa.'

'But people in the clinic know—'

'My brother will handle them. As a family we are very close.'

Abby sucked air into her lungs and tried to think logically. 'It doesn't make sense.'

'It makes perfect sense.' He contradicted her smoothly. 'I cannot have more children so I am determined to have Rosa, but I can see now that she also needs her mother. We will be a family.'

'But not a real family.'

He gave a careless shrug. 'This is the twenty-first century. The word "family" has achieved rather a broad definition.'

'And what do I get from marrying you?'

One dark eyebrow lifted mockingly. 'You get Rosa, and a lifestyle beyond your wildest dreams.'

'I don't have dreams about lifestyle,' Abby said flatly. 'There's more to life than money.'

Her time at school had taught her that. She'd been surrounded by the daughters of the rich and famous and she'd seen at first hand the problems that they'd often had to deal with. Nico's extreme wealth was one of the reasons they were currently hiding out in his apartment.

'If you don't want it for yourself, then think about what it would mean to Rosa. At the moment she is living in a damp, cramped little flat and soon you won't have anywhere to live at all. I still don't understand why you chose to have Rosa in such an unconventional way but, whatever your reasons, can you really deny that she'd be better off with two parents?'

Abby stared at the floor and blinked back tears. He was clever, she had to hand it to him. He'd discovered her weaknesses and was using the one argument that he knew would win her over. She'd never been hung up on the lack of money, knowing that such things weren't important to a child. But she'd always felt guilty that Rosa didn't have any family other than her. Most especially she didn't have a father.

And that was her fault.

She was painfully conscious of the fact that she'd taken the decision to go ahead and have a child on her own, but now she was being offered the chance to give her daughter a normal family life.

She almost laughed at her own thoughts. As if she had a choice! Nico had made it clear that he was taking Rosa anyway. The only choice she was being given was whether to go with her daughter. As his wife.

So what was her problem?

She should have hated him for threatening to take Rosa, but the truth was that she didn't. Part of her could even understand why he'd behaved the way he had. The knowledge that he was unable to father a child must have been almost unbearable for such a proud Italian male. It was hardly surprising that he'd gone after Rosa. He wanted a child and she knew all about wanting children.

And there was no doubting his love for his daughter. Even offering to marry her was driven by his love for Rosa. He genuinely believed that the child would be better off with two parents and was willing to sacrifice himself for that belief.

Abby bit her lip.

And that was the problem, of course. He was sacrificing himself. There was no love or affection involved. It would be a marriage of convenience.

Abby glanced at him surreptitiously, taking in the tangle of dark curls visible at the neck of his shirt. He was one hundred per cent virile male and the thought of being married to him, of spending time with him on a regular basis, made her struggle for breath.

But it wasn't going to be a physical relationship, she

reminded herself. It was purely a business arrangement. A marriage for the benefit of Rosa. And although she was suspicious of wealth, could she really deny Rosa the chances that money could buy her or the opportunity to have a loving, extended family?

Totally distracted, she watched while Rosa fed herself the pasta, using a mixture of fingers and spoon, spreading some of it on her face and some of it on the table.

If she'd expected Nico to be fazed by a messy toddler, she was disappointed.

He watched with quiet amusement as Rosa attacked the food with chortles of delight, and then finally fetched a cloth to clean her up.

She had to hand it to him, he was impressive. Even the antics of a mischievous toddler didn't threaten that legendary cool.

'I'm sorry about your kitchen floor,' Abby muttered, suddenly realising just what a mess her daughter had made of his pristine, hand-painted kitchen. There seemed to be splodges of Bolognese sauce everywhere.

'I'm delighted that she enjoys pasta so much,' came his calm reply as he lifted the little girl out of the chair and carefully wiped her face and hands. 'She is clearly more Italian than English. My mother will adore her.'

She studied him curiously, thinking how human he could be at times.

'Are you due back at the hospital?'

'Tomorrow.'

'Have the staff seen the papers?'

She hated the thought of the staff gossiping.

'Of course. Which is why we need to make a decision about the future.'

'If I married you—what would happen?' She bit her lip nervously, hardly able to believe she'd even asked the question.

'You and Rosa would come and live with me here,' he

said immediately. 'I would finish my contract with the hospital and then we would move back to Italy.'

'You want us to live in Italy?'

'*Sì*—of course.' Nico nodded, clearly surprised by her question. 'It is my home. I travel for my work, but my base is Italy. I have homes in Milan and Rome, a ski lodge in Cortina and my family owns a villa in Sardinia. All my family are in Italy. Rosa's family. I want her to be near them and I want her to speak Italian.'

'But if I married you—if we pretended that we—' She broke off, finding the conversation impossibly difficult. 'I mean, Lucia would know the truth. And Carlo. They both know that we never had a relationship. That Rosa was—'

'You can safely leave them both to me.'

'And there's another thing.' She flushed deeply and he lifted an eyebrow.

'Go on.'

'I just don't think we could be convincing. No one in their right mind would believe that you'd fallen for me.' She hugged herself with her arms, hideously self-conscious. 'I mean, look at me! I'm just a nurse, Nico. I'm not exactly the sort of girl that you usually wear on your arm.'

He frowned at her as if the thought hadn't occurred to him before, and then he reached forward and jerked the elastic band out of her ponytail, letting her blonde hair fall softly over her shoulders.

'What are you doing?' She clutched at it, painfully aware that she'd been up all night with Rosa and hadn't had time even to comb her hair. She must look an absolute fright.

'I would certainly never date a woman with her hair in an elastic band,' Nico said dryly, his aim perfect as he tossed the offending article into the bin. 'As for the rest—although you seem totally unaware of the fact, you have a stunning face and figure, *cara mia*. No red-blooded male, seeing you on my arm, will have any trouble seeing why I married you.'

A stunning face and figure?

Abby gaped at him. Nico Santini thought she was *stunning*?

Something shifted inside her and she looked at him closely, but he merely returned her gaze steadily, nothing in those fabulous dark eyes giving the slightest clue as to what he was thinking.

Abby stared at him helplessly, feeling completely trapped. If she said yes, it meant spending the rest of her life in close proximity to someone who drove her to a permanent state of nervous tension, but Rosa would gain a family. If she said no, she would lose Rosa.

And that just wasn't an option that she could ever contemplate.

'All right,' she said in a small voice, not meeting his eyes. 'I'll marry you if it means that I can stay with Rosa. But it's a business arrangement only.'

'Agreed.'

Without a flicker of emotion he rose to his feet in a fluid movement and picked up the phone. 'I'll make arrangements for us to be married here in the next couple of weeks and then we'll go home to Italy for our honeymoon.'

Honeymoon.

The kitchen suddenly felt hot and airless and Abby took a gulp of air and concentrated on cleaning up Rosa.

It wouldn't be a real honeymoon, she reminded herself quickly.

He was just taking her to meet his family.

It was a holiday really. Something that she and Rosa had never had together because such an option was well outside her tight budget. She should be looking forward to it.

So why did she feel as though she was entering the lion's den?

Abby stayed at Nico's apartment for another three days until she was sure that Rosa had recovered sufficiently to go back to the crèche. During that time she rarely saw Nico, although his staff were incredibly attentive.

Giovanni, the chef, took the time to discover her favourite foods and Rosa adored him from the first moment, eating everything he put in front of her with a messy enthusiasm that clearly delighted him.

Matt, the bodyguard, was always nearby, his broad-shouldered bulk a constant reminder of the life she was taking on.

It was he who vetoed her plan to take the bus to work on her first day back.

'Are you trying to get me fired? I have worked for the Santini family since I left the army,' he told her, 'and they are excellent employers. I have no wish to put my job at risk.'

'Surely the press won't be looking for me on a bus,' she reasoned, and he gave her a pitying look that answered her question.

'No bus,' he told her firmly, his eyes sympathetic. 'Nico's orders. If you want to go anywhere, you go in the limo.'

'The limo!' She gaped at him. 'But that's ridiculous! I can't turn up at work in a limo! I'm just a nurse.'

'You're also Domenico Santini's fiancée,' Matt reminded her dryly. 'And Rosa is his daughter. There's no way she's going anywhere without protection.'

'Well, what happens when we get to work? Am I allowed to put her in the crèche?'

He nodded. '*Sì.* We have run a thorough security check on the staff and Nico is satisfied that she is as safe there as anywhere. And she clearly enjoys the company. And, anyway, I will be around.'

Abby looked at him. 'Around?'

'Yes, I'll be around the hospital,' he said evasively. Abby wondered how on earth she was going to get any work done with all this going on around her.

'Does this often happen to Nico? The press chasing him?' How did he even begin to live a normal life?

Matt gave a wry smile. 'Only when he is seen with a new woman. The female hearts of Europe flutter briefly, hoping that it will be fleeting. I expect there'll be some serious disappointment when they read about you.'

And surprise, too, Abby thought wryly. She was hardly his type of woman.

'But I need to go to the flat to pick up more of Rosa's things,' she said lamely, and Matt held out his hand.

'Give me a list and the keys. I'll sort it.'

Abby sighed and reached for some paper and a pen. She'd known Nico long enough to know that it wasn't worth arguing.

They arrived at the hospital in comfort and Abby had to admit that it was bliss not to have to wrestle with bus queues and toddlers first thing in the morning. She slipped self-consciously out of the limo and slid into work as discreetly as possible.

Heather waylaid her as soon as she arrived on the ward.

'Is it true?' Her eyes were alight with curiosity and excitement. 'Are the papers correct? You had a fling with Nico Santini?'

Abby gave a wan smile. 'I…er…yes, it's true that Rosa is his child.'

She couldn't quite bring herself to say they'd had a relationship. Despite what Nico thought of her, she was extremely truthful by nature.

Hopefully everyone would still draw the right conclusions if she admitted that Rosa was his child.

'You are such a dark horse!' Heather looked stunned. 'You didn't even tell us that you knew him.'

'I was at school with his sister.'

'But you never told him you had his baby.' Heather was looking at her dreamily. 'But he came to find you and now you're getting married. That's *so* romantic.'

Romantic?

Abby pinned a smile to her face and wondered how on earth she was going to keep this up. She glanced around the ward, which was humming with activity. 'I can see we're busy. Where do you want me? I'm really sorry I've been off for the past few days.'

'No problem. We were worried about Rosa, but Nico kept us informed. He's been remarkably human to the staff since he announced that he was marrying you. You obviously bring out the softer side to him.'

No. It was Rosa that did that, Abby thought regretfully. She had no effect on him whatsoever.

'OK, what's been happening since you were here last?' Heather checked her notepad. 'Thomas Wood is still doing well, his wound is clean, his sats are good and he's on free fluids. You look after him as you've got such a good relationship with them. If he carries on like this, he'll be going home in another few days.'

'What happened to baby Hubbard?'

'I spoke to his mother that night Rosa was sick and she was happy to take the baby home. Jack did the balloon atrial septostomy and that improved her oxygen saturation so she's gone home and she's being readmitted in two weeks for her op.' Heather broke off as the ward doors opened and a medical team pushed a cot towards her. 'Oh, this is my new admission. Little boy born by Caesarean section in the night. He was very breathless and can't feed and the paediatrician was worried that he has a congenital heart defect, although he couldn't hear a murmur. Jack arranged for him to be transferred and he and Nico are going to review him together.'

She walked towards the team. 'You can put him in room six for now. Abby, can you bleep Jack and Nico and tell them that baby Hopcroft has arrived? Where's the mother?'

'Still on the ward,' the nurse told her. 'She's having her drip and her catheter out and then they've told her she can come up in a wheelchair. I ought to warn you, she's totally devastated that something is wrong. The sooner someone tells her what's going on the better.'

'Of course.' Heather listened while they finished the handover and then turned to Abby. 'If the mother is distraught, this is a good one for you. You're always brilliant with worried parents. You're so calm.'

Calm?

Abby gave a wan smile. After everything that had happened to her in the past week she didn't think that she would ever be calm again. She certainly didn't feel calm. She felt as though her insides were hosting a major hurricane.

She and Heather had only just finished settling the baby when Jack, Nico and a large number of junior doctors walked onto the ward. The group included the paediatrician who had referred the child.

'I was called to Theatre because it was a section,' he told the other doctors, briefing them on the history. 'The child was full term and there were signs of foetal distress but the baby was breathing hard from the moment he was born and in my opinion he was blue.'

Nico was watching the baby. 'Did the mother have ultrasound during her pregnancy?'

The paediatrician nodded. 'Yes. Two, but there was no evidence of a problem.'

Nico frowned. 'Any family history of congenital heart disease?'

'Not that I could discover, but I had some trouble getting any sense from her. The mother was distraught.'

'Understandably so.' Nico began to examine the tiny baby. 'His respiratory rate and effort are increased,' he murmured, moving the cot sheet down so that he could feel the pulses in the baby's feet. 'And his pulses are diminished.' He turned to Abby and for a brief moment she thought she saw something flicker in that dark gaze. Then it was gone and he was totally professional again. 'Could you do a four-limb blood pressure, please?'

Abby nodded, aware that a lower blood pressure in the legs was indicative of a congenital heart defect.

She pressed the button on the dinamap and recorded the pressures.

Nico nodded as he looked at the results. 'He has a lower blood pressure in the legs and weak femoral pulses. Also, his liver is enlarged and his lungs are congested. What is his oxygen saturation?'

Abby checked the monitor quickly. 'Eighty per cent.'

'Which is consistent with cyanosis.'

The paediatrician moved closer. 'I thought I detected a systolic murmur, but I could have been wrong.'

'You weren't wrong,' Nico said smoothly as he finished his examination. 'Well done. It isn't always easy to hear.'

The paediatrician looked stunned at the praise and then grinned as if he'd won the lottery.

Abby looked at Nico with helpless fascination. Until she'd started working with him she'd seen him as Mr Cool, so totally in control of his emotions that even a smile didn't see the light of day unless he'd planned it. But she couldn't have been more wrong.

She'd seen the warmth that he was capable of showing with worried parents, with Rosa and now with a colleague, and she was rapidly coming to the conclusion that there wasn't a person in the world that he couldn't charm if he wanted to. She was beginning to understand how Lucia could have adored her brother so much. The combination of masculine strength and human kindness was a potent cocktail that was devastatingly attractive. No wonder women went crazy about him.

The paediatrician was still looking at Nico. 'So what's your diagnosis?'

Nico didn't hesitate. 'I will want to see a chest X-ray

and an echo, but in my opinion he has a coarctation of the aorta.'

Abby listened carefully, knowing that a coarctation of the aorta was when the main artery taking blood around the body was narrowed, hence the lower blood pressure in the legs.

The paediatrician let out a breath. 'The mother's going to be distraught. She was hoping it was nothing.'

'Of course she was,' Nico said coolly. 'This is her baby—naturally she wants him to be completely healthy. I will speak to her when she arrives on the ward.'

'So what will happen now?'

Nico answered without hesitation. 'We will give him Prostin to reopen the ductus and that will improve the oxygen saturation. At the same time we will stabilise the circulation with fluids and dopamine. Once he is stable we will operate.'

'And what does that involve?' The paediatrician was losing no opportunity to question Nico but he didn't seem to mind.

He described the operation in detail and even invited the other doctor into Theatre to watch.

Abby watched him work, her mind only half on what he was saying. The other half was trying to get to grips with the fact that she was going to marry this man.

She'd been aware of a few curious glances from members of the medical team but Nico had behaved in his usual cool, detached manner, nothing in his behaviour indicating that they had anything other than a professional relationship.

'Stop drooling over him,' Heather murmured in an undertone as she walked past, and Abby gave her a shocked look.

Drooling?

Was that what people thought?

She certainly wasn't drooling. She was wondering what on earth she'd agreed to.

It was almost the end of her shift when Nico strode up to her, an ominous expression on his handsome face.

'Matt has just returned from your flat.'

She stared at him blankly, wondering why that would cause him to look so angry. 'And?'

'And he had the pleasure of meeting your landlord.'

Abby swallowed. 'Oh.'

'Yes, oh.' Nico's tone was low so that they couldn't be overheard. 'Why didn't you tell me that he was threatening you?'

'I— He wasn't— I didn't—'

'Abby, I know the truth,' Nico said flatly, a frown touching his dark brows. 'Matt pretended he was renting you a flat and the guy warned him not to expect any favours from you. He boasted to Matt that he'd put the rent up to get you out after you refused to sleep with him.'

Abby winced. It sounded so sordid, put like that. 'It wasn't that great a flat anyway,' she said lamely, and Nico gave a groan and raked his fingers through his dark hair in a gesture of pure male frustration.

'Why the hell didn't you tell me the truth? You let me think that you'd got behind with the rent, that you couldn't manage your finances, instead of which—' He broke off and took a deep breath.

'It really doesn't matter,' she mumbled, and he gritted his teeth.

'Abby, it does matter. You should have said something.'

'You wouldn't have believed me,' she pointed out, astonished that he should be so bothered by it. 'You were determined to take Rosa from me and you'd made up your mind that I was a bad mother and terrible with money.'

'Instead of which, you were being bullied and exploited,' he growled. He closed his eyes for a moment and exhaled sharply. 'I misjudged you and I apologise. If it is any consolation, I regret it immensely and I truly wish you had tried to tell me the truth. I like to think I would have listened.'

She stared at him, stunned.

Nico Santini was *apologising* for having misjudged her?

And that wasn't the only thing he'd misjudged her on, of course, but she knew better than to touch on the subject of Rosa's paternity again. Instead, she gave him a faltering smile.

'It doesn't matter.'

'*Dio*, it does matter. You are a single mother, struggling on her own. You were vulnerable and he took advantage.' Anger and distaste burned in the depths of his dark eyes. 'If it is any consolation, I doubt that he'll be doing the same thing to anyone else.'

Abby's eyes widened as she digested the implications of his last sentence. 'What did Matt...?'

Nico's mouth tightened. 'Matt seems to have grown quite fond of you over the past few days. He was furious and he can be quite intimidating when he's crossed.'

A pacifist by nature, Abby flinched at the thought of Matt so angry but then she remembered just how badly the landlord had frightened her and decided that Matt had probably done everyone a favour.

Suddenly a thought occurred to her.

'So I presume that's the end of my flat?'

'Of course.' He spoke with complete certainty, his tone autocratic. 'There is no way I would allow you to return there and, anyway, you have no need for a flat any more. We're a family now and your home is with me.'

Their eyes locked and her heart suddenly bolted.

Her home *was* with him.

But losing the flat made it seem even more final.

She no longer had anywhere to run if things didn't work out between them.

CHAPTER SIX

AT THE hospital Thomas Wood was finally discharged home and Lorna gave Abby a big hug.

'I really, really don't think I would have survived it if you hadn't been here. I can never thank you enough.'

Abby returned the hug. 'It was nothing—I'm just glad he's all right. Now, are you sure that you're happy about everything?'

Lorna nodded. 'I've got an appointment with the cardiologist in two weeks.'

'But if you're worried about anything at all in the meantime, you know you can call us.'

Lorna cuddled Thomas closer. 'When will his chest heal?'

'It takes about six weeks,' Abby told her. 'Try and avoid lifting him under the arms because that can make it sore.'

'OK.' Lorna glanced around the ward. 'Is Nico around? I really wanted to thank him again before we left.'

'He's in Theatre, but I'll pass on your thanks.'

Lorna gave an awed smile. 'I read in the papers about the two of you. Wow! You are one very lucky girl.'

Abby forced a smile.

Was she?

Lorna was obviously determined not to let the subject drop. 'The papers said that you were getting married—is that true?'

Abby nodded, resigned to the fact that everyone in Britain seemed to know everything about her life in minute detail.

'We're getting married soon,' she said vaguely, not liking to admit that Nico hadn't given her a date. All he'd said was that it would happen quickly.

In the meantime she was living in his apartment, being cooked for by Giovanni and chauffeured everywhere by his driver, while Nico spent most of his time at the hospital.

'I wasn't expecting to have to take time off while I did this job,' he'd explained to her on the first evening. 'I will arrange cover for us to have a week in Italy so that you can meet my family, but in the meantime I have a ridiculous workload to get through. I apologise for not being able to spend more time with you and Rosa.'

It was true that his schedule was punishing and it was a tribute to his stamina that he managed to keep up with the volume of work without any visible evidence of strain or pressure.

Abby didn't mind the fact that she only ever saw him on the ward. It made her life easier and more relaxed.

What worried her was what was going to happen when they had to spend a week in each other's company.

Ten days after Abby had moved into his apartment, Nico's driver and Matt collected her for the journey to work but drove in the opposite direction from the hospital.

'Where are we going?'

Matt kept glancing out of the rear window. 'To meet Nico.'

'But the ward—'

'Nico's arranged it all.'

Abby felt her stomach turn over and almost laughed at her own reaction. How on earth was she going to cope with being married to the man when the mere mention of his name had her reacting like a cat on hot bricks?

They drove through the centre of London and then the chauffeur pulled up on a double yellow line and Matt opened the door.

'Go straight inside without looking left or right,' he ordered. 'I think we've managed to fool the press but you can never be sure.'

'But...' Abby glanced at the elegant building and then at her daughter who was fast asleep, her dark lashes a perfect half-moon against her pale cheeks.

'I'll take care of her,' Matt said immediately, placing a reassuring hand on her shoulder.

Abby hurried up the steps and into the building, stopping on the threshold as she saw Nico standing there, dauntingly male and impossibly broad-shouldered in a dark grey suit.

'Rosa?'

'Asleep in the car. Matt said he'd take care of her.'

Nico gave a brief nod of approval. 'She has a tiring journey ahead of her. The sleep will be good for her.'

Abby looked at him. 'Journey?'

'We're getting married,' he said briefly, his footsteps echoing as he led her across the marble hallway.

She stopped dead and gaped at him. 'Getting married? Now?'

He lifted an eyebrow. 'You have changed your mind?'

'N-no,' she stammered, trying not to notice just how much her legs were shaking. 'Can I at least comb my hair?'

'Of course.' His smile was amused. 'I have also bought something for you to change into.'

He strode with casual assurance along an elegant corridor and flung open a set of double doors.

'Where is this place?' She glanced around her in confusion, noticing the comfortable sofas and the magazines stacked on the low table. 'It looks like someone's house.'

'It's a hotel.'

'A hotel?' She stared at him blankly. How could it be a hotel? From the outside the building had nothing to draw attention to it and she'd seen no staff.

'It's a very exclusive hotel,' he murmured, clearly reading her mind. 'People come here when they wish to be assured of discretion. You have twenty minutes before the ceremony.'

She glanced around the room and for the first time noticed the white silk dress hanging from a rail by the window.

'You bought me a dress? What if it doesn't fit?'

'It will fit.' His eyes ran over her in a totally masculine scrutiny which left her skin burning and her pulse racing. 'The rest of your wardrobe will be sent to the villa. I'll check on Rosa.'

The rest of her wardrobe? Without giving her a chance to question him further he strolled out of the room and left her staring after him.

Realising that she had very little time, she glanced at her watch in dismay and then reached for the dress.

It was fabulous and when she glanced at the label she almost dropped it. Knowing that it must have cost a small fortune, she hardly dared to put it on. But, then, Nico Santini was in possession of a very large fortune, she reminded herself dryly. Even a dress like this wasn't going to make a dent in his bank balance.

Two minutes later she was staring at herself, open-mouthed in amazement.

The dress fitted perfectly. In fact, a bit too perfectly.

It skimmed every contour of her body, showing her tiny waist and the womanly curve of her breast and hips.

He hadn't even laid a finger on her and yet he'd guessed her size exactly. But, then, he'd had plenty of experience with women, she reflected wryly.

Why did that thought give her butterflies in her stomach?

Abby bit her lip as she looked in the mirror. If Nico thought he was marrying a stick insect, he was in for a severe disappointment.

Scooping up her wild, wavy hair, she fastened it to the top of her head with a silver pin.

She'd just finished applying make-up when Nico and Matt strolled back into the room with Rosa.

'Wow!' Matt gave her an approving smile and then caught Nico's frosty gaze and subsided with a murmur of apology.

Nico released Rosa's hand and walked across to her, releasing her hair from the pin and nodding approval as blonde curls cascaded down her back.

'Much better,' he drawled, his eyes sliding with disconcerting thoroughness over her silk-clad body. 'And now we should be getting on. We have a schedule to keep.'

Abby sat on the plane and tried to get a grip on her emotions which were fast spiralling out of control.

The simple ceremony had gone smoothly, witnessed by Matt, one of the staff of the hotel and Rosa, who had sat on the floor with her thumb in her mouth throughout.

Nico had repeated his vows in his usual clear, cool voice, whereas her voice had been barely audible.

And all the time she'd been aware that the wedding was merely been a tool for Nico to take possession of Rosa.

And take possession he had, she thought miserably as she stared out of the window of the private jet. Rosa was asleep again and Nico was working on his laptop, the jacket from his suit slung over the back of his seat and the top button of his shirt undone.

He looked thoroughly male and wickedly handsome and she wondered how on earth they were going to convince his family that they were a couple. He hadn't so much as touched her hand since the registrar had proclaimed them married.

And she should be grateful for that, she told herself firmly.

Fortunately, at that moment Rosa awoke and needed attention, which prevented Abby from dwelling on the evening to come.

By the time they arrived in Sardinia, Abby was exhausted and Rosa was fractious and difficult, crying persistently as they were hustled into the car.

'We are nearly there,' Nico murmured, reaching into his pocket and producing a small toy for Rosa, which stemmed the tears for a short time. 'She must be very tired, poor thing.'

Abby gave a faltering smile, relieved and touched that he'd understood that Rosa's behaviour was the result of tiredness.

All the same, she was grateful when they finally arrived at their destination, pulling up outside a beautiful villa on the edge of a golden sandy beach. The sea shimmered temptingly in the late afternoon sunlight and in the distance a flotilla of boats sailed across the bay.

Abby gasped in delight, her own tiredness temporarily forgotten. 'What a beautiful place!'

'I'm glad you approve.' Nico's light drawl held a hint of amusement. 'It is our retreat from the smog of Milan and it's certainly a pleasant change from the East End of London.'

It certainly was.

Abby stared at the sand longingly and had to fight the urge to slip off her shoes and run into the sea.

'It looks deserted. There's no one on the beach at all.'

'That's because it's private,' he informed her dryly, and she blushed, embarrassed by her own naïvety.

Of course it was private.

The Santini family would hardly share a beach with tourists, would they?

The next half-hour was a whirl of introductions and shrieks and incomprehensible Italian as Nico's mother and extended family welcomed him home.

Where did Nico get his ice-cool approach to life? Abby wondered in amazement as she watched his warm and affectionate mother fussing over Rosa and his grandmother smiling benignly from a comfortable rocking chair.

She'd been expecting his family to be reserved and undemonstrative, instead of which they couldn't have been more welcoming.

'You will call me Francesca. And you should know that this is the happiest day of my life,' Nico's mother told her, enveloping Abby in a warm hug which brought a lump to her throat. 'You have done what I thought no woman could do. You have captured my Domenico's heart.'

Abby closed her eyes briefly, wondering what on earth Nico had told them all. She felt a stab of guilt that they were deceiving this woman.

'Two years ago, his life was so black,' Francesca told her in a low voice, aware that Nico was within earshot. 'He had that terrible illness...' She broke off with a shudder. 'But he was lucky and they cured him. But he thought he would never have children, until he found out about you....'

No. He'd found out about Rosa.

Abby smiled weakly. 'Yes...'

'And you should have told him you were pregnant,' Francesca scolded lightly, taking Abby's hand and patting it gently. 'My Domenico is an honourable boy. He would have done the right thing straight away and then you wouldn't have been apart for two years. You would have been there for him when he was ill, instead of which he shut us all out—'

Nico said something sharp which Abby didn't understand, but his mother subsided instantly and took Abby's arm.

'Nico tells me I'm interfering so I will be quiet now. Why don't I show you to your room and you can get washed and changed for dinner? You must be exhausted after the flight.'

'Is my father joining us?' Nico loosened his tie and poured himself a drink.

Francesca shook her head. 'He intended to, but he had to fly to Paris last night.'

Nico's eyes narrowed. 'He works too hard.'

'It is a family trait,' his mother replied quietly, giving him a meaningful look which he accepted with a grudging smile.

'And Carlo?'

'Carlo is already here and Lucia is planning a brief visit, too. Now, enough of that. Poor Abby must be overwhelmed by meeting all these new people. I've put you in the Beach Room.' Francesca turned to Abby with a smile. 'You'll love it. We had it decorated quite recently. There is a wonderful balcony which opens up onto the deck and the little one can sleep in her own room just down the corridor. I've employed a nanny to take care of her so that you can have a complete rest. If there's anything else you need, you only have to ask.'

Abby returned the smile, completely charmed by Nico's mother. Lucky Lucia, she thought wistfully as she followed her upstairs to her room. No wonder she'd always longed for the holidays.

She frowned slightly, wondering whether Lucia had been told about their wedding. Did she even know that Nico had tracked her down?

Hoping that the meeting wasn't going to be awkward, Abby took a shower and changed for dinner then checked on Rosa, who was tucked up fast asleep in the pretty nursery. A uniformed nanny was folding her clothes in a neat pile.

'Good evening, *Signora*.' Fortunately she spoke good English. 'I'm Chiara. I will be Rosa's nanny while you are here—it will give you a chance for some rest.'

Her eyes gleamed slightly and Abby gritted her teeth. There was no mistaking the implication and it wasn't anything to do with rest.

As it was, she knew that she was going to have plenty

of time to spend with her daughter but she didn't think it was sensible to argue that fact at this point. Instead, she checked Rosa quickly, thanked the nanny politely and made her way to her room.

A maid was unpacking two suitcases full of clothes that Abby didn't recognise.

'Signor Santini asked me to unpack,' the maid said respectfully, and Abby opened her mouth and closed it again. Clearly this was what Nico had been referring to when he'd said that he'd bought her a wardrobe.

She should have protested, but part of her felt like a child in a sweet shop confronted by such a variety of tempting outfits. Whoever had done the shopping had chosen well.

She selected a pretty dress, left her hair loose and made her way downstairs for dinner.

Nico was standing by the fireplace, looking relaxed and impossibly handsome, the sleeves of his dark linen shirt rolled back to reveal tanned forearms. His jet-black hair was still wet from the shower and Abby found herself wondering where his room was. Obviously nowhere near hers, which was all that mattered.

His gaze skimmed over the dress and there was no mistaking the masculine appreciation in those stunning dark eyes. 'You look wonderful, *bella mia*.'

Blushing frantically, she accepted a drink and shook hands with Carlo, whom she'd never met before but warmed to instantly.

Although physically there was a strong resemblance between the two brothers, Carlo had none of Nico's cool reserve, his gaze warm and welcoming as he introduced himself to Abby.

Although they'd never met in person, he had been instrumental in arranging for her treatment at the clinic but not by a flicker of an eyelid did he betray that he knew who she was.

It was clear that the two brothers were close and the conversation around the table was lively and interesting.

Halfway through dinner her eyelids started to droop and Nico frowned at her across the table.

'You are exhausted, *cara mia,*' he said quietly, his dark eyes narrowed as they scanned her pale face. 'No one will mind if you want to go upstairs.'

She smiled at him gratefully, surprised by his perceptiveness.

She *was* tired. All in all it had been a pretty stressful day.

Deciding to follow his suggestion, she excused herself and made her way up to the bedroom, took a leisurely bath and then changed into one of her new nightgowns.

It was ridiculously glamorous and revealing, but fortunately no one was going to see it except her, she reflected as she adjusted the thin silk spaghetti straps.

This nightie was designed for sin and passion, not warmth and comfort. It was fortunate that the nights were going to be extremely warm in Sardinia.

She snuggled down into bed, feeling instantly drowsy, but then she heard the click of the door and sat bolt upright, her heart thumping as Nico strolled in, his jacket slung carelessly over one shoulder.

Abby clutched the sheet to her chest, her eyes wide. 'Wh-what are you doing in here?'

'What do you think I'm doing?' He tossed the jacket onto a chair and started undoing the buttons on his shirt, his expression faintly amused. 'I'm going to bed with my wife.'

Abby stared at him, appalled. 'You have to be joking.'

One ebony brow lifted. 'Why would I be joking?' The shirt landed next to the jacket and her mouth dried as her eyes caught a glimpse of broad male chest covered in curling dark hairs.

Dear God, he was undressing in her bedroom....

'Wait a minute.' She looked at a point just behind him so that she didn't have to look at his body. 'We don't have that sort of marriage....'

He frowned. 'What other sort of marriage is there?'

'You know what I mean!' She clutched the sheet tighter. 'Ours is a business arrangement. Security for Rosa.'

'Precisely.' He stepped out of his trousers, revealing a pair of black silk boxer shorts. 'Security for Rosa means a happy marriage. And as far as I'm concerned, a happy marriage means plenty of sex.'

Sex?

She had a brief glimpse of hard, muscular thighs before dragging her gaze away.

'But I don't even really know you....' Her voice was strangled and a smile slashed across his male features.

'After tonight you will know every inch of me, *cara mia*.'

She shook her head, unable to grasp that he was serious. 'I— This isn't what I...' Inspiration struck. 'You can see other women! I wouldn't mind.'

'*I* would mind,' he said smoothly, his tone mildly amused. 'Anyway, I have too high a profile to be able to be seen with different women. It would cause gossip. Especially among my own family. We are newly married, *cara mia*, they expect us to share a room.'

Abby looked around the room, her heart tumbling in her chest. 'Well, in that case you could sleep on the sofa.'

'I'm six feet three,' he reminded her in a low, masculine drawl. 'If I sleep on a sofa, I'll never walk again.'

'Then *I'll* sleep on the sofa.'

The amusement vanished from Nico's eyes. 'You'll sleep in the bed.' There was no mistaking the command in his tone. 'With me. You married me. Sex is part of marriage.'

'We don't have to have sex just because we're married—plenty of couples don't have sex.'

He looked at her with blatant incredulity. 'If you are

suggesting that I can do without sex, you certainly have a great deal to learn about me. I'm Italian, *tesoro*. I have a high sex drive.'

The tip of Abby's tongue sneaked out and moistened her lower lip. She didn't even want to think about his sex drive. 'But you—we—don't love each other.'

He threw back his head and laughed in genuine amusement. 'I have never loved anyone, *cara mia*. Fortunately for you, my performance in bed isn't affected by the lack of that fabled emotion.'

She stared at him, heart pounding. 'You really think you're the ultimate lover, don't you?'

A smile slashed across his handsome face. 'I'm Italian, *angelo*. Making love is the one thing we know how to do really, *really* well. But first we need to—what's that phrase you have in English—set a few ground rules?' He lifted a hand and smoothed a finger down her cheek. 'Firstly you need to start looking at me. It is hard to build a relationship with someone who won't look at me. You look at the floor, or the ceiling, or my tie when I wear one—just about anywhere except my eyes.'

Nico lifted her chin firmly and gave a slight smile as she lifted her eyes to his. 'Better. Much better. Secondly, you need to stop being so jumpy when I walk into the same room as you. I want you to relax when you are with me.'

Relax?

Her heart was beating so fast she thought it might burst through her chest. She could no more relax with him than she could with an escaped tiger.

His dark eyes were lazily amused. 'This is the first time in my life I've had a woman asking me to sleep on the sofa rather than in her bed. This is a totally new experience, *tesoro*,' he drawled softly, 'and a not altogether flattering one.'

'—I'm not interested in flattering you,' she stammered. 'I married you because I wanted Rosa and because we agreed that two parents would be better for her than one. We don't have a relationship. We both know that I'm not your usual type of woman.'

'That is partly true…' His eyes narrowed and he looked at Abby speculatively as if he'd just realised something. 'Which makes it all the more interesting that the chemistry between us is so powerful.'

Chemistry?

She gaped at him in astonishment and then shook her head. 'I don't know what you mean. There's no chemistry.'

'Are you really so naïve that you can't see it?' He looked at her, stunning dark eyes raking her pale features. 'Why do you think I make you so nervous?'

'Because you're an autocratic bully,' she said immediately, too shaken by the direction of the conversation to be shy with him. 'You scare me.'

'That's not true. It is your feelings that scare you,' he said softly, his husky male voice torturing her nerve endings. 'There is a strong sexual charge between us. Go on, Abby, admit it,' he murmured thickly. 'You have often looked at me and wondered how I make love.'

Heat pooled in her belly and she shook her head in frantic denial, shaken by her body's reaction to his explicit statement.

'You're just so impossibly arrogant that you can't believe that there's a woman out there that doesn't want you.'

He sat down on the bed next to her and his male scent teased her nostrils.

Looking everywhere except at his powerful body, she tried to scoot across the bed but he stopped her with one lean, brown hand, leaning across her so that her means of escape was blocked.

Her heart was pounding. 'Don't you understand "no"?'

'Perfectly. But you haven't said it,' he said huskily. 'When you do, I'll stop.'

She opened her mouth to say it and then froze with shock

as Nico's mouth descended on hers. The touch of his lips against hers was nothing like she'd expected. Instead of hard, he gave her soft, instead of rough, he gave her gentle, using every ounce of expertise to tease a response from her.

Fire burned deep in her stomach and she placed a hand against his muscular chest, intending to push him away. But instead she felt his weight pressing her back onto the bed as he came down on top of her, his mouth never breaking contact with hers.

He lifted a hand to her face, stroking her cheek gently as he used his tongue to trace the seam of her lips and dip seductively inside.

Suddenly she was surrounded by Nico—his scent, his taste, his weight, and his incredibly skilled touch.

His mouth still on hers, he slipped the straps of her nightie down her arms, and she felt the hair on his chest graze her exposed nipples. Then he lifted his head and looked down at her, his breathing not quite steady.

Instinctively Abby lifted a hand to cover herself, but he caught her wrists in his hands and she felt her cheeks burn with embarrassment under his heated scrutiny.

'You are impossibly shy,' he murmured gently, his Italian accent suddenly pronounced, 'and yet you have a stunning figure, *angelo*. You are full of surprises. Who would have thought that hidden under that nurse's uniform is the body of a goddess?'

A goddess?

Totally thrown by his comment, Abby lay still, barely breathing, fascinated by the expression in his eyes. He couldn't stop looking at her, his eyes dark with a primitive need as his eyes fastened on her pink nipples.

'You have the most incredible breasts....' he groaned, sliding down the bed so that his head was level with that part of her. For endless moments he hesitated, staring down at the soft roundness without trying to conceal his hunger.

Then he lowered his head and drew one nipple into the heat of his mouth and Abby gasped as sensation shot through her. She forgot about the fact that she barely knew him, she forgot about being nervous or shy. Instead, she arched towards him, instinctively seeking more.

When he finally lifted his dark head his breathing was decidedly unsteady, and he looked at her nipple, now glossy and wet from the touch of his mouth. Then he lifted his eyes to hers.

'Are you saying no?' His voice was husky and heavily accented and she shook her head, mute, her body a mass of sensation.

With a satisfied smile that was pure, conquering male, he lowered his head to her other breast and subjected it to the same treatment while he tortured the other with the tips of his fingers.

She writhed and arched underneath him, trying to free her body of the almost intolerable pressure he was creating inside her.

He continued his relentless assault on her breasts, his free hand sliding up her back and teasing the soft silk down her body. Suddenly she was naked except for a pair of silk panties and he slid further down the bed, kissing his way down her body until he reached the most private part of her.

'Nico!' She tensed with shock as she felt his mouth touching her through the flimsy silk and she tried to push him away but he gave a soft laugh and held her thighs apart. 'I want to know every part of you Abby. Every single part…'

'Nico, please…' She gave a sob of embarrassment which turned to a gasp of disbelief as he swiftly dispensed with her panties and used his tongue to caress her most intimate place.

Embarrassment was replaced by a sensation so exquisite that she thought she'd explode.

He used his mouth until she was writhing and shaking and then he lifted his head and slid up the bed to cover her with his powerful body.

She stared up at him, dazed, her blue eyes feverish. 'Nico...'

She couldn't believe what she'd just let him do.

'No more shyness, *cara mia*,' he purred softly, his dark eyes burning into hers as he used his fingers where his mouth had been. 'Soon there will be no part of you that I don't know intimately.'

The ache between her thighs was intolerable and suddenly she was desperate to have him there, where she needed him most. Frantically she pushed at his silk boxer shorts, sliding them down the hard muscle of his thighs so that he was left as naked as her.

'*Io voglio te...*' he groaned in Italian, and she looked at him dizzily, her body totally outside her own control.

'I said that I want you,' he muttered huskily, and she shivered underneath him as she felt him take her hand and guide her towards him, encouraging her to touch him with the same intimacy that he'd touched her. Her fingers stroked him gently and she just had time to register his size and power before he was parting her thighs and positioning her under him.

She stared up at him, her breath coming in shallow pants as she waited for the touch that she craved so desperately.

The tension between them had built to such an intolerable level that she didn't expect him to pause, but he did, lifting a hand and stroking blonde curls away from her face with fingers that weren't quite steady.

'I'll try and take it slowly but I'm not promising. You excite the hell out of me, *cara mia*,' he groaned huskily. 'You are so full of surprises. All shyness on the surface and passion underneath.'

Abby arched against him, begging with her body.

She didn't want slowly.

She just wanted *him*. And she didn't care if he hurt her.

Even so, his first thrust stretched her beyond her expectation and she gasped and tensed, her fingers curling into his back.

Nico paused and spoke softly to her in Italian and although she didn't understand, she felt herself relax.

His dark eyes hot with passion, he slid a strong arm under her hips and then entered her fully, thrusting deep into the heart of her.

She could hardly breathe, all rational thought suspended by the excitement which exploded inside her body. He controlled her utterly, building the rhythm until he created a sensation so exquisite and extreme that she cried out his name and moved against him in a frantic attempt to ease the almost intolerable tension that he'd created within her body.

His love-making was fierce and possessive and he drove them both to a state of fevered ecstasy until finally she crashed over the edge in a climax so intense that she cried out in disbelief, holding tightly to him as she felt the powerful thrusts of his completion.

Held securely in his arms, Abby closed her eyes, savouring the incredible closeness and the weight of his powerful body on hers. She never wanted the feeling to end. She wanted him to hold her for ever.

But he didn't.

Instead, he shifted his weight and looked down at her, a strange expression in his dark eyes.

Abby lay still, her eyes locked with his, totally shocked by the feelings that had erupted inside her.

What was he thinking?

What had it meant to him?

Afraid to speak in case she severed the incredible connection between them, she lay quiet, waiting for him to make the next move.

And move he did.

Muttering a soft curse in Italian, he lowered his mouth to hers again and Abby ceased to worry about what was on his mind.

CHAPTER SEVEN

ABBY awoke the next morning to find the sun blazing through the window and no sign of Nico.

Glancing at the clock, she gave a gasp of horror. How had she slept so late?

Hot colour burned her cheeks as she remembered the night before. It was hardly any wonder she'd slept so late. Nico had made love to her for most of the night and when eventually she'd fallen asleep, she'd been physically and emotionally exhausted by the intensity of the experience. For the first time in her life she'd felt truly close to someone. Remembering how she'd snuggled into his arms in the aftermath of their love-making, she gave a groan of embarrassment and covered her face with her hands.

How could she have even pretended to herself that she didn't find him attractive? The man was devastating and one flash of that electric smile had sent her into a tailspin from which she'd never recovered.

And now she had to face him.

Shrinking with shyness after the way she'd responded to him, she dressed quickly and made her way down to the terrace where the family seemed to take their meals.

They were all sitting around the table, talking and laughing as they enjoyed breakfast, and Rosa was in a high chair, beaming happily at her grandmother, her uncle and her father.

'Good morning.' Nico rose to his feet as she hesitated on the edge of the terrace, and Abby wished she could vanish into the background.

Her whole body tensed as he strolled towards her, her

cheeks flaming pink as she remembered the liberties he'd taken with her body the night before.

'If you don't look me in the eyes, everyone will guess what we spent the whole night doing,' he said softly, his voice husky and slightly amused. 'You have no reason to be embarrassed, *angelo*.'

Warily her eyes lifted to his and she saw speculation flicker on those dark depths. He must have had virtually no sleep and yet he looked totally rested. The man's strength and stamina were awesome.

'Come and have some breakfast.' He took her arm and guided her back to the table, pulling out a chair and seating her between Rosa and himself.

'She is a wonderful child, Abby, and a credit to you,' Francesca said warmly as she handed Rosa another piece of bread to eat. 'She is so happy and friendly. Nico tells me she goes to a crèche.'

Nico frowned slightly and Abby braced herself to defend her decision, but surprisingly enough Carlo spoke up, his voice calm and measured.

'And a good thing, too. That's probably why she's so sociable.' He threw an amused glance at his brother. 'And we all know that the more germs children pick up early on the healthier they are as they grow older.'

Nico gave a grudging smile and Abby looked at Carlo gratefully. 'My friend runs it,' she said quickly, 'and she's known Rosa since she was born, so she isn't with strangers.'

Francesca tutted. 'You must have struggled so much, trying to manage with a child on a nurse's salary. You should have contacted my Nico straight away to tell him you were pregnant.'

Abby coloured but before she could think what to say Nico had spoken to his mother in rapid Italian, his expression forbidding.

His mother pulled an apologetic face and looked at

Abby. 'I'm so sorry. Nico tells me off for interfering and he's right. Now, then, what are you going to do with your day?'

Abby glanced longingly at the beach which seemed to start at the bottom of the garden.

'I'd love to take Rosa to the beach,' she said shyly. 'She's never seen the sea before.'

'Perfect!' Francesca beamed approvingly. 'The three of you will spend the morning on the beach and when the sun gets too hot you'll come back up here for lunch and a siesta.'

Siesta.

Abby caught Nico's eye briefly and then looked away in embarrassment as she read the amusement and something else in his gaze. There was no doubting what he planned to do during the siesta and it certainly wasn't sleeping.

'Do you have everything you need?' Francesca poured herself more coffee. 'A bikini? A costume for Rosa? You must wear a hat. You are so fair you'll burn badly in our heat if you don't cover yourself up.'

Abby smiled at her, touched and warmed by her consideration. 'I have a hat, thank you,' she said, lifting a napkin and wiping the jam from Rosa's face.

'You must make sure you rest on the beach,' Nico's mother said firmly, handing Rosa another piece of bread to chew. 'You must be so tired after everything that happened yesterday. I cannot believe my Nico whisked you away and married you with no warning. He can be very overbearing at times. And none of us were able to be there.'

Nico was glowering at his mother but she continued regardless. 'Nico does not know how to be romantic. He is too impatient with such things.'

Carlo glanced at his mother. 'Stop stirring,' he warned gently, and she pulled a face.

'I just cannot believe he got married without inviting us.'

She turned to Abby again. 'What about your family—were they there?'

'That's enough.' Nico's tone was sharp but Abby put out a hand and smiled at his mother.

'My parents are both dead,' she said quietly, and Francesca closed her eyes briefly, clearly mortified.

'You poor thing—I didn't know.' She glared at Nico and then looked back at Abby with concern. 'But family is not just about parents—you must have aunts, uncles, grandparents?'

Abby gave a self-conscious shake of her head. 'I—I don't have anybody except Rosa,' she stammered quietly, and everyone around the table fell silent, all eyes fixed on her.

Nico was suddenly still, an odd expression in his eyes.

Finally Francesca spoke, her voice troubled. 'Nobody?'

'Nobody.' Remembering the years of loneliness, Abby gave a shaky smile and felt a lump building in her throat.

Did Nico have any idea how lucky he was, having such a fabulous family?

Francesca was staring at her in dismay. 'My poor girl...' She rose from the table and enveloped Abby in an enormous hug. 'Then it is doubly wonderful that you met my Domenico because you can no longer say that you have nobody. You have him and all of us.'

Did she?

Abby returned the hug and then risked a glance at Nico, but his expression was unfathomable, his dark eyes hooded as he surveyed her across the table.

She stared back at him in helpless fascination, appalled at the intensity of her own feelings.

One night.

That was all it had taken. One night in his bed and she was totally lost.

What a complete idiot!

She'd done the one thing he'd said that he didn't want from her. She'd fallen in love with him.

She dropped her eyes to her plate, afraid that he'd read the truth in her gaze.

How could it have happened?

How could she have fallen in love with a man who'd threatened to take her daughter from her?

Because she understood now what had driven him to such extreme lengths, and she sympathised with those emotions. And if his macho, controlling personality had shocked her to begin with, he'd more than redeemed himself since with his behaviour towards their daughter. He didn't seem bothered if she was fractious or tired, he still enjoyed her company.

Abby closed her eyes and faced the inevitable. She'd seen Nico Santini at his worst and she'd still fallen in love with him. She loved his strength and his ferocious intellect, she understood that his emotional detachment concealed an ability to feel deeply, but most of all she loved the vulnerability that she sensed was there but which pride prevented him from acknowledging.

Which meant that she was in trouble because he certainly didn't love *her*. She wasn't fooled by the closeness they'd shared in the bedroom. To a man like Nico, sex was something completely separate from love.

Nico had married her to gain possession of Rosa and for no other reason.

Why would he fall in love with her? No other woman had been able to hook him and if she thought that one night of enjoyable sex would be enough to make her different then she was fooling herself.

So what was she going to do?

Living in a marriage of convenience was one thing, but what happened when one of them broke the rules and fell madly in love? Abby swallowed hard and stared down at her hands.

Clearly thinking that she was upset about her past, Carlo reached over the table and touched her hand. 'We're all delighted that you're now part of our family,' he said quietly, the concern in his eyes visible evidence that he was all too aware just how close she was to tears. 'And now perhaps you two should get on the beach before it's too hot for Rosa.'

With a brief nod of gratitude to his brother, Nico rose to his feet and lifted Rosa out of her high chair and into his arms.

'I asked the nanny to put her things together,' he told Abby as they strolled back into the villa. 'You just need to change yourself and then we can go.'

He looked down at her with a slight frown. 'You're very pale, *angelo*. Are you feeling all right? My mother can be very tactless sometimes. If she upset you—'

'She didn't upset me,' Abby interrupted him quickly, keen to change the subject in case he guessed the real reason for her misery. Nico was the cleverest man she'd ever met. She had no illusions about his ability to work out just exactly what was wrong with her, given enough time.

'You are sure?' Still looking at her, he suddenly lifted a hand and freed her hair from the clip she'd used to restrain it.

'Nico…'

'You have stunning hair,' he breathed, the heat in his vibrant dark eyes a reminder of the intimacies they'd shared the night before. 'Don't wear it up again unless you are at work.'

With that parting shot he strolled back towards their room, leaving her staring after him, wondering what was happening to her. She was so affected by him, so starving for every morsel of attention, that she was ignoring the fact that he was behaving like a caveman.

By rights she ought to twist her hair into the tightest knot possible just to annoy him, but she knew that she wasn't going to do that. More likely she was going to wear her hair loose for the next fifty years.

You're pathetic, she told herself hopelessly as she followed him back to their room. One night in his bed and you're falling over yourself to please him.

But the incredible intimacy they'd shared the night before had unlocked something inside her that she'd kept buried since childhood. Fear of rejection and her mammoth insecurity had kept her from forming relationships and trusting another human being. Making love with Nico had changed all that.

Now she could think of nothing that she wanted more than to be intimate with Nico Santini for the rest of her life.

Chiara met her outside their room, carrying a bag stuffed with Rosa's belongings.

'I think I have remembered everything.' She smiled. I even found a bucket and spade.'

Abby thanked her, took the bag and slipped into their room to get changed, grateful that Nico was in the bathroom so that she could do it without an audience.

She pulled a pretty blue cotton sundress over a bikini that left virtually nothing to the imagination and remembered to pack a hat in the bag.

'Ready?' Nico strolled out of the bathroom, wearing shorts and a loose T-shirt which fell softly over the muscles of his broad shoulders.

Treating herself to a glance at his incredible body, Abby felt her whole body heat and quickly bent down to pick up the bag.

'Shy again, Abby?' His deep voice teased her and she glanced up with a wry smile.

'It's you,' she muttered, her eyes sliding towards the door. 'You turn me into a nervous wreck....'

'But at least we're joking about it, which is a start.' He

traced the line of her jaw with a strong finger and looked at her thoughtfully. 'Come on. Time to go.'

They settled themselves on the sand a few minutes later and Rosa plopped down on her bottom, delighted by her new environment.

'Now, bang the bottom of the bucket, like that. Good girl.' Abby laughed as Rosa beat the bucket with the spade and the sand plopped out in a perfect shape. 'There you are—castle.'

Rosa chuckled and bashed the sand with the spade until it was totally flattened.

'She likes the beach,' Nico said smiling indulgently, as Rosa stabbed the sand with the spade.

'Do you think she's all right?' Abby looked at him anxiously. 'Not too hot?'

Nico shook his head, his dark eyes narrowing as he looked at her. 'The reason you are finding it hot, *tesoro*, is because you refuse to remove your dress,' he drawled, and she hugged her knees self-consciously.

'That's because the clothes you arranged for me only include bikinis that aren't designed for swimming,' she muttered, and his eyes gleamed.

'Did you like them?'

She gave him a shy smile. 'You were very generous. Thank you.'

'*Prego*. As we've established that you like the clothes, there really is no logical reason for you to keep your dress on. I saw every single inch of your body last night,' he reminded her in husky tones, his eyes amused, 'so, in the circumstances, your shyness is misplaced. And if you are worried that I will be unable to control my baser urges, I assure you that I am not in the habit of making love to a woman with my entire family watching from the villa.'

Abby glanced behind them, realising that the beach was clearly visible from the terrace.

'I'm taking Rosa for a swim.' Nico rose to his feet and

dragged off his shirt and then bent to scoop Rosa into his arms.

Abby stared after them as they walked across the sand. The sea sparkled in the burning sunlight as though someone had thrown a million diamonds into the waves.

It looked thoroughly inviting and suddenly she decided that he was right. She was being ridiculous. Pulling the dress over the head, she applied sun cream liberally and then walked gingerly across the hot sand to the water's edge.

Nico was up to his waist in the water, dipping a giggling Rosa into the sea and then lifting her high into the air.

Abby watched them with a smile and then suddenly Rosa noticed her and babbled excitedly, straining towards her mother.

Nico turned and saw her, his eyes wandering thoroughly over her body as she paused with her toes in the water.

'It's a good job the water's cold,' he said dryly, a slight smile touching his mouth as his eyes rested on the tempting curve of her cleavage. 'You have a fabulous figure, *angelo*. Now, come into the water and have some fun.'

And they did have fun.

They played in the waves with the toddler and when Nico thought that Rosa had been in the sun for long enough, they retreated back to the sand where umbrellas shaded their towels.

'This is so wonderful…' Abby turned to him with a smile to find him watching her intently.

'You like my home? After the inquisition from my mother at breakfast, I was afraid you might be wishing for privacy,' he drawled, adjusting Rosa's hat so that she wasn't in the sun.

Abby shook her head. 'I love your family,' she said quietly, 'and I think you're very lucky.'

Nico gave a wry smile. 'Well, I apologise again for my mother. She interferes terribly.'

'She didn't upset me, and I think it's great that she interferes,' Abby said wistfully. She would have given anything for parents who loved her so much that they'd want to involve themselves in her life.

'I knew your parents were dead but I didn't realise that you had no other family,' Nico said gruffly, settling himself on the towel next to her and leaning back on his elbows. His dark chest hair glistened with sea-water. 'I am beginning to understand why you went ahead and had Rosa, even though you were so young.'

Abby remembered the searing emptiness of her life before Rosa and stared bleakly into the distance.

'I always envied Lucia,' she said quietly. 'Not because of the money but because of her family. Whenever something happened at school, one of you turned up to support her. School plays, sports days—whatever it was, she always had someone there cheering her on. And it was often you.'

Nico shrugged. 'Our father was often too busy running the business.'

'But one of the family was always there for her.'

Nico gave a wry smile. 'I'm not sure that she was always as grateful for my presence as you seem to think she should have been. She thinks I'm overbearing.'

'I think you love her,' Abby muttered. 'I would have given anything for someone to care enough about me to tell me off.'

'Would you?' Nico's voice was disturbingly gentle. 'Tell me about your parents.'

Abby hesitated. She wasn't used to confiding in anyone. All her life she'd been on her own and it didn't come naturally to broadcast her feelings.

'It's pretty boring really,' she muttered, and he reached out a hand and lifted her chin, forcing her to meet his disturbingly direct gaze.

'Not boring. We are married now, *angelo*,' he said softly. 'I told you last night that I wanted to know every single part of you. That includes what is inside your head. No secrets, Abby.'

She swallowed. 'My parents both had big careers. They were appalled when they had me but fortunately for them boarding schools provided the answer. They seemed to think that as long as they put me in the best school, they could forget about me. So that's basically what they did.'

Nico frowned ominously, his disapproval evident. 'You must have been unbelievably lonely. I understand why you were determined to have Rosa.'

Abby stared at the sand. 'I *was* lonely. In fact, there was never a single moment in my childhood when I didn't feel lonely,' she admitted, wondering why she was telling him things she'd never even admitted to herself before. 'I always hoped that once I became a nurse my parents would be proud of me, but nothing changed and they died within six months of each other before I finished training.'

'And that was when you decided to have Rosa?'

She stared across the sparkling sea. 'I was always desperately maternal and I wanted a child so badly I was willing to contemplate anything. Whatever you may think, I didn't go into it lightly. I was worried that I was depriving her of a father but I managed to convince myself that one good parent was better than two indifferent ones.'

'I'm surprised that you didn't just rush into marriage with the first guy who asked you,' Nico drawled, his gaze disturbingly intense. 'What happened to Ian?'

Her head jerked towards him and she stared at him, eyes wide. 'How did you—?' She broke off and her slim shoulders sagged slightly. 'Oh, of course, I'd forgotten you hired a detective. You know everything about me.'

Sea-water clung to his thick, dark lashes and his jaw was dark with stubble. He looked sinfully handsome and she felt her stomach lurch in response to the lazy look in his eyes.

'Not everything,' he said smoothly. 'Detectives can give

you the facts but not the reasons. Why did you get engaged so quickly? Were you trying to create a family?'

She hesitated and then nodded, curling her toes into the sand and making patterns with her feet. 'Yes, I was,' she said honestly. 'I met Ian and he seemed really keen on me…' She broke off with a wry smile and his eyes narrowed.

'But?'

'A month before our wedding I discovered that he was already married. He never intended to marry me. Apparently I was just one of many.'

Nico's eyes narrowed. 'That must have hurt.'

'Well, the worst of it was, it didn't really,' she admitted. 'When I found out about his wife, apart from feeling very sorry for her I was just hugely relieved that I'd found out what a louse he was in time. I suppose I didn't really love him. I was just hideously lonely and loneliness makes you do stupid things.'

'Perhaps you confused lust with love, *tesoro*,' Nico drawled softly, and she gave an emphatic shake of her head.

'No. It definitely wasn't that. We hardly ever— I mean, I didn't really— I assumed I wasn't that keen on sex, but after last night I know—' She broke off, her face scarlet with embarrassment at the confession that he'd just managed to drag out of her.

He reached out a lean hand and tilted her face to his in a gesture of pure male possession. 'After last night you know differently.'

His husky voice and the look in his eyes scorched her flesh and for a long moment she stared at him, memories of shared intimacy pulsing between them. Then she jerked her chin away from his fingers.

'You are still so incredibly shy with me, *cara mia*,' he murmured, his tone amused. 'And if he was your first and only boyfriend, I'm beginning to understand why. You have a lot to learn about being relaxed with a man.'

'You don't help,' she blurted out, hating the way he made her feel. Hot, panicky—desperate for him to kiss her again. 'You're always so cool....'

'Not cool,' he murmured, leaning towards her, his breath warm on her heated flesh. 'Definitely not cool.'

'They can see us from the house,' she breathed, mesmerised by the look in his stunning dark eyes.

'I'm not touching you,' he drawled softly, his eyes dropping to her full mouth. 'I'm just cranking up the heat, ready for our siesta. I haven't finished talking to you yet. There is much, much more I want to know about you.'

'Oh.' She looked at him dizzily. He had a voracious appetite for sex and the knowledge of what he could make her feel had a devastating effect on her concentration.

'So you weren't upset over Ian?'

Running her tongue over her lips, she dragged her eyes away from his tanned, muscular shoulders and tried to drag an answer from her drugged brain.

'I—I was upset because it meant that I couldn't have children straight away.'

Nico looked at her quizzically. 'And that had been your plan?'

She nodded. 'I wanted an instant family. If I could have gone to a shop and bought one, I would have done it.' She gave a long sigh. 'And I suppose that's what I did in effect. I confided in Lucia and she suggested I talk to Carlo. At first it all seemed completely ridiculous, but then I started thinking, Why not? I convinced myself that plenty of children grow up in single-parent households with estranged parents sharing them and fighting over them. Would a child born to one parent who loved her deeply be so badly off?'

Nico frowned. 'You didn't just think of waiting a few years until you found a man you fell in love with?'

'I suppose I didn't have any faith that it would happen.' *But it had.* She was in love with Nico. And now they were married with a baby. The irony of the situation wasn't lost on her but, of course, that was one observation she could never share with him.

'So that's when you decided to have Rosa?'

'Well, it wasn't quite as easy as that, but basically, yes.' Abby reached for her dress and pulled it over her head, freeing her blonde hair with her hand so that it tumbled down her back. 'Lucia made all the arrangements for me. She was a real friend.'

Nico was watching her through veiled eyes and she wondered what he was thinking.

'Rosa's getting pink cheeks,' she said suddenly, kneeling up to gather their things together. 'I'm going to take her back to the villa.'

Without waiting for him to reply, she swept Rosa into her arms and started to make her way back up the beach.

She really didn't want to talk about Rosa's conception.

It just reminded her of the precarious nature of their marriage.

CHAPTER EIGHT

BACK in their room Abby showered quickly before joining the family for lunch on the terrace.

The table was laden with delicious food, bowls of shiny black olives, freshly grilled fish, salads and interesting breads.

Wine flowed as freely as the conversation, and by the time lunch ended Abby felt her eyelids drooping. She'd had virtually no sleep the night before and was feeling drowsy in the hot sunshine.

Noticing her predicament, Nico stood up and stretched out a hand, glancing round the table as he pulled her to her feet. 'If you will excuse us, we are going for a siesta.'

Abby smothered a yawn. 'But Rosa—'

'Chiara will take her for a nap,' Francesca said immediately, waving a hand towards the cool villa. 'Go, and we don't expect to see you until dinner, and not even then if you're too tired to join us.'

Once in their room, Nico pulled her deliberately in his arms and lowered his head. His kiss was hot and demanding and her insides felt scorched by the sensation that he aroused in her. Her lips parted and he cupped her face in his strong hands, exploring every inch of her mouth with his.

She felt the cool brush of soft cotton against her bare legs and back and then he had swiftly removed the dress, leaving her clad only in her bra and silk panties.

He backed her towards the bed with his powerful body, supporting her as she tumbled onto her back, a look of totally male satisfaction simmering in his dark eyes.

'I have been wanting to do this all morning,' he murmured huskily, removing her underwear with a speed that made her gasp with shock.

'Nico, it's broad daylight.'

'So?' Amusement slashed across his handsome face as he looked down at her body with an earthy groan. 'You are absolutely stunning, *cara mia*. It would be such a waste to only make love to you in the dark. I want to see every inch of you.'

Totally in control, he bent his dark head, taking one of her peaked nipples in his mouth and caressing it with maddening skill.

Burning between her thighs, she arched towards him and he lifted his head and rolled onto his back, taking her with him.

Her blonde hair trailed onto his chest and he lifted a strand with a hand that wasn't quite steady.

'I love the way you tremble when I touch you and I love the fact that you honestly have no idea how sexy you are,' he groaned, dragging her head down and kissing her deeply.

Abby felt the thickness of his erection against her own wet heat and she gasped as he lifted her with strong hands and positioned her to take him inside her.

'Nico…' Her cry of shock turned to a sob of ecstasy as he entered her in a smooth thrust, his body stretching and dominating hers even though she was supposedly in the position of control.

'You are mine now,' he murmured against her mouth, his touch fiercely possessive. 'You belong totally to me.'

Flushed and gasping for air, she felt her body move automatically to follow his lead, felt herself surrender to his powerful demands until the tension exploded inside her and she fell against him, her hot cheek resting on the tangled hair of his chest.

Briefly she felt his hand stroke her hair away from her

face and then he rolled her onto her back and slid down her body.

'Nico…' Her voice was an embarrassed squeak as he parted her thighs, his intention clear. 'You can't. It's the middle of the day….'

'Which makes it all the more exciting, *angelo*,' he breathed.

By the time the seduction was complete, Abby was too stunned to move. Nico had made love to her in positions that she'd never even imagined and done things that had brought hot colour to her already permanently flushed cheeks.

A look of intensely male satisfaction on his stunningly handsome face, Nico leaned across and kissed her swiftly before coming to his feet and prowling over to the bathroom.

'Sleep well, *tesoro*,' he murmured, the expression in his dark eyes lazily amused as they slid over her drained and sated body.

Through a haze of sex-induced stupor, it occurred to her that he should have been tired, too, but he certainly didn't look it. But that was Nico all over, she thought sleepily, her eyelids drifting closed even before he'd strolled into the bathroom. He had more stamina than the rest of the world put together.

The week passed in a haze of sociable meals, trips to the beach and wild love-making. Nico had a remarkable knack of getting her to open up to him and she found herself telling him things that she'd never told anyone before in her life and the closeness she felt from those confessions just fuelled her deepening love for him.

'What about you?' she said one day, after she'd finished telling him another secret of her life. 'I want to know you, too.'

He gave her a wolfish smile that was pure, predatory male. 'You are beginning to know me extremely well, *cara mia.*'

Abby blushed hotly at his husky implication. It was certainly true that he made very sure that she knew exactly what he needed in bed. 'You know I didn't mean that. I mean you never talk to me about how you feel....'

'I feel extremely content,' he said lazily, lying back in the sun and closing his eyes. Thick black lashes rested on his incredible cheek-bones and she looked at him shyly.

'Did you never think of getting married before?'

He gave a slow smile, his eyes still firmly closed. 'I never had a reason to.'

Abby's own smile faded and she felt as though she'd been showered with cold water. Of course he hadn't. The reminder that he'd only married her to gain possession of Rosa and give his daughter a family left her feeling miserably depressed.

'But did you plan to have children?'

'Of course. I'm Italian.' His voice was rough and he kept his eyes closed. 'All Italian males want a family. I just assumed I'd be able to have them whenever I was ready.'

'And then you were diagnosed with cancer?' She faltered slightly, bracing herself for rejection. His mother had made it obvious that he'd never talked about his illness with anyone. Why did she think he might talk to her? Just because she'd trusted and confided in him endlessly over the past few days, it didn't mean that he was obliged to do the same.

There was a long silence and then he gave a sigh and covered his face with a tanned forearm. 'That diagnosis was the biggest shock of my life. At first my fertility was the last thing on my mind. I just wanted them to treat it as aggressively as possible, but then once they were convinced that they'd done everything they needed to do I was suddenly faced with the reality of not being able to have children.'

'That must have been awful.' Her voice was soft. 'I can understand why you came after Rosa.'

His eyes flew open and he propped himself up on his elbows, looking at her through wickedly thick lashes the colour of dark chocolate.

'For a few very bleak months I thought I would never have a child of my own.' He gave a humourless laugh. 'That knowledge is not easy for any man to cope with, but for an Italian male it is particularly hard on the ego.'

Abby held her breath, aware that such an admission from him was an amazing step forward.

'Did you talk to anyone about it?'

Nico shook his head. 'Of course not. It was something I had to come to terms with myself and I have to admit I had a few very low months. I worked myself to the bone as a means of distraction and there wasn't a day that I didn't think about the child that I'd fathered. I told myself that I couldn't interfere but it nagged at me so badly that I thought I'd at least check what had happened to the child.'

Abby bit her lip and felt suddenly sick. 'Nico, about—'

'I don't want to talk about that,' he interjected smoothly, as he pulled her towards him. 'It's history now and I really couldn't care less about what happened at the clinic. At one point in my life I had given up on ever being a father in the real sense of the word. To find myself living with my daughter is a miracle that I would have paid any price to achieve.'

'Even marriage,' she joked shakily, and he dealt her a lingering smile that made her toes curl.

'Being married to you definitely has its compensations, *cara mia*,' he said in a husky voice, and then the talking stopped and he rolled her over and pushed her down onto the blanket.

Nico glanced down at Abby's sleeping form, shaken to the core by the unfamiliar feelings that swamped his normally logical brain.

When he'd embarked on this relationship, he'd been prepared to pay any price to gain possession of his daughter, even marriage.

It had never occurred to him that making love to Abby would turn his world inside out.

It was just sex, he told himself firmly, standing up in a fluid movement and pulling on a robe. And what he needed was fresh air to clear his head.

Without waking her, he opened the French doors that led to the terrace and strolled noiselessly out into the night air.

Just sex.

Glancing back into the dimly lit bedroom, his eyes narrowed at the sight of her blonde hair tangled over the pillow and wandered appreciatively over the pale curve of her hip.

Sucking in his breath he dragged his gaze away and faced the truth.

It wasn't *just sex* at all.

With her warmth and her generosity, Abby had curled her way around his heart. She'd even persuaded him to talk about the subject that he avoided with everyone else. *His infertility.*

And somewhere between meeting her and making love to her he'd even ceased to care that she'd deceived him. With a childhood like hers, who could blame her for grabbing any opportunity that had come her way?

He rubbed a hand over the back of his neck to relieve the tension, grimly aware of the irony of the situation.

He'd never fallen in love with a woman before and when it had finally happened it had to be with someone who didn't love him and was never likely to.

Nico swallowed a groan of frustration. He was only too aware that she'd married him for her daughter's sake.

Was there any way he could persuade her to fall in love with him?

* * *

Abby was curled up asleep on his chest that night when she heard Rosa crying.

Still half-asleep, she went to move but he stopped her, tucking the sheet around her and dropping a kiss on her head.

'You are exhausted, *tesoro*. Go back to sleep. I will see to her.'

Thinking that sharing parenthood very definitely had its advantages, Abby went back to sleep and enjoyed a completely undisturbed night.

When she awoke the next morning there was no sign of Nico and she padded next door to Rosa's room, astonished to see him trying to change a nappy.

Rosa was twisting and wriggling and refusing to co-operate, and he was muttering something in Italian as the tapes of the nappy stuck to his arm.

He glanced up and saw her in the doorway, frustration written all over his handsome face.

'*Dio mio*, how do you get a nappy near her?' He looked at her with naked incredulity. 'She won't keep still.'

Abby grinned and walked across the room. 'She thinks it's a game.'

'Some game,' Nico growled, admitting defeat and handing her the clean nappy. 'This is the second one I've wrecked. I am prepared to be a very hands-on father, but even I have my limits.'

Abby was hiding her amazement. She never, ever would have thought that a man like Nico, the original macho male, would have even contemplated changing a nappy.

'What's happened to Chiara?' Abby smoothed the nappy out, grabbed Rosa's ankles and snapped the tapes together before the toddler had time to squirm.

'I sent her away, but I won't make that mistake again,' Nico murmured, amusement simmering in his eyes as he watched the efficient way she completed the task that he'd struggled with. 'You do that with amazing speed and efficiency. I'm totally floored with admiration, *cara mia.*'

'You sent her away?' Abby scooped Rosa up into her arms and looked at him questioningly.

Colour touched his cheek-bones and for the first time she noticed the heavy stubble on his jaw and the lines of tiredness around his eyes.

'Rosa had a very disturbed night,' he said through gritted teeth. 'I think she's teething.'

Abby frowned. 'I remember hearing her cry and you getting out of bed to see to her. I don't remember you coming back.'

'That's because I didn't,' Nico said dryly. 'I never would have thought that someone so small could cause so many problems. She refused to go to sleep unless I was holding her, and as soon as she drifted off and I tried to put her back in the cot, she woke up again.'

Abby smothered a smile. 'You should have called me or let Chiara take over.'

Something flickered in those dark eyes and he looked away from her, concentrating his attention on his daughter. 'I couldn't sleep,' he muttered, his Italian accent more pronounced than usual. 'Just remind me never to do the night shift if I'm operating the next day. I can survive on very little sleep but I have just discovered that it does have to be in one go. Last night I had about three hours in snatches of eight minutes at a time.'

Abby laughed. 'It's torture, isn't it? They always say that the person who invented the phrase "sleep like a baby" had never actually had one.' Her smile faded and she touched his arm gently. 'You're a brilliant father,' she said softly, 'and Rosa is a very lucky girl.'

There was an electric silence and an odd expression flickered across his face, but before she had time to interpret the look Nico gave a groan and took her mouth in a devastating kiss. His tongue explored the interior of her mouth in a kiss so explicit and intimate that she moaned in protest when he finally lifted his head. If she hadn't been holding Rosa she knew that he would have made love to her there and then in the nursery.

'Give Rosa to Chiara,' he instructed, his breathing unsteady as he looked at her with flattering appreciation. 'I might be prepared to forfeit sleep for my child, but I've decided that a whole night away from my wife is asking too much.'

Two hours later Abby sat at the breakfast table, totally dazed by the intensity of Nico's love-making. For a man who'd been up all night, he certainly didn't suffer on the energy front, she thought, feeling her cheeks grow pink as he strolled across the terrace to join the family.

Considering he didn't love her, she couldn't fault him. He was totally attentive to her every need, he listened and confided and as for their love-making… She breathed in unsteadily. Well, maybe it was just sex to him, but when they were in bed together she had no trouble pretending that what they shared was real. He might not love her but she knew how much he wanted a family. Surely that should be enough for her?

'I hear the little one had a bad night,' Francesca fussed over Rosa and the little girl beamed at her happily, banging the table with her cup and threatening everyone with jammy fingers.

They'd almost finished breakfast when there was a sudden bustle inside the villa and Lucia breezed out onto the terrace in a waft of dark hair and expensive perfume.

'Surprise! I'm a day early.' She stopped dead when she saw Abby, her eyes widening in amazement. 'Abby? What are you…?'

Her gaze flickered to Rosa and then Nico, and suddenly her smile faded and her face lost its colour.

'You told me you'd met someone,' she whispered, her

eyes fixed on Nico's face. 'You told me you wanted to introduce me to your wife.'

'And so I do,' Nico replied calmly. 'But I don't suppose you need much in the way of introductions. You already know Abby.'

Lucia looked at her friend in confusion and Abby immediately got to her feet and gave her friend a hug.

'It's really great to see you,' she murmured, and Lucia returned the hug, her eyes flickering to Carlo and then to their mother.

'You should have told us you were coming early,' Francesca reproved. 'You shouldn't be taking taxis. Tell her, Nico.'

Nico's eyes rested on his sister, noting her pallor. 'I think Lucia is old enough to make her own decisions on such things,' he drawled softly. 'She's more than able to think through the consequences of her actions.'

Abby gave a start, wondering if there was a hidden meaning behind his words.

Lucia obviously thought so, too, because she suddenly looked distinctly nervous.

Francesca rose to her feet, oblivious to the tension simmering around the table. 'I'll go and tell Maria that we're one extra for breakfast.'

She vanished into the villa and Lucia turned on her brother, visibly nervous. 'How did you—? I mean—'

'How did I discover your little deception?' Nico's tone was chilly. 'Simple really. I decided to follow up the child I fathered. Remember the one, Lucia? The child of your thirty-eight-year-old friend and her infertile husband?'

Lucia winced and threw a pleading glance at Carlo who sighed and rubbed a hand across his jaw.

'Nico—'

'It's fortunate for you that this story has a happy ending,' Nico said evenly, his eyes still fixed on his sister. 'I now have the family I wanted. What you and Abby did is history. I don't want it mentioned again.'

'But Abby didn't do anything,' Lucia said shakily. 'I was the one who persuaded you to be the donor. Abby didn't know anything about it.'

There was a frozen silence around the table, and even Carlo seemed beyond speech.

Groaning inwardly, Abby stared down at her plate, waiting for the inevitable explosion.

It was a long time in coming. The silence built and built until Lucia's discomfort and anxiety were felt by everyone.

When Nico finally spoke his voice was deceptively calm. 'Are you telling me,' he said softly, 'that Abby had no knowledge that I was the father?'

Abby held her breath and put the fork she was holding back down on her plate.

'Look, it really doesn't—'

Nico lifted a hand to silence her, his dark eyes fixed on his sister's flushed face.

'Well, of course she didn't.' Lucia threw her brother a look of disbelief. 'She never would have chosen you. That's why I didn't tell her. Abby was about the only girl in school who *didn't* fancy you. She's always been terrified of you, that's why I'm so amazed that she agreed to marry you and—'

'That's enough, Lucia,' Abby said shakily, interrupting her friend quickly before her indiscretion could create any further damage. 'As Nico says, it's all history now. Let's forget it.'

Nico's eyes were still on his sister, his tension pronounced. 'I assumed she knew.'

'Oh, my God…' Lucia paled visibly as the truth hit her. 'You bullied her into marrying her, didn't you? You thought she'd *wanted* you as the father of your child.'

His handsome face ashen, Nico rose to his feet. 'Are you seriously telling me that this was all your idea?'

'Yes.' Lucia's confession was little more than a whisper and Nico switched languages, his eyes fixed coldly on his sister's crumpling face as he spoke in rapid Italian.

Abby couldn't understand a word of it but Lucia burst into tears and there was a sudden tension in Carlo's broad shoulders.

'Nico, please...' She put out a hand and touched his arm gently and he broke off and drew in a shaky breath, clearly battling to regain control of his temper.

'Why?' He glared at his sister. 'What made you do it?'

'Because I thought you were the greatest,' Lucia sobbed. 'I adored you, Nico. You were the very best big brother a girl could have, and when Abby said she wanted a baby, I couldn't think of a single person in the whole world who'd be better than you.'

Nico closed his eyes and let out a long breath. '*Dio*, I don't believe this.'

'I knew you wouldn't agree to father the child of a young girl so I lied to you. I didn't mean any harm. I didn't think you'd ever find out.' Tears poured down her cheeks and she lifted a shaking hand to her mouth. 'I certainly didn't think you'd bully Abby into marrying you. I can't believe you did that. She's terrified of you.'

She was crying so hard now that Abby stood up and went to her, instinctively wanting to comfort her friend.

'No one bullied anyone. Please, don't cry. It really doesn't matter,' she said softly, slipping her arms around the other girl and holding her close.

'Of course it matters.' Lucia rubbed away the tears with the back of her hand and gulped. She glared at her brother, her eyes filling again. 'I always thought you were the cleverest person I knew but obviously you're not. Anyone can see that Abby isn't the sort of girl who lies. She's gentle and good and horribly shy with men. How could you even *think*—?'

'Because that's what you led me to think,' Nico interjected, his tone harsh. 'You told me that you drew up a list of qualities you were looking for in a father—'

'We did,' sobbed Lucia, 'and then *I* decided that you were the best match. *Me*, Nico. Not Abby. I never told Abby. She was totally innocent. You have to let her go. You can't do this!'

Nico's face was a mask, his features expressionless as he faced his sister across the table.

Then he said fired something at her in Italian and she gave another sob and ran into the villa.

Abby made a move to follow her but Carlo put a hand on her arm. 'I'll go to her and I'll deal with Mamma,' he said quietly, consternation in his eyes as he looked at Nico. 'You two have things to discuss.'

He left the table and Abby stared down at her hands, totally at a loss. What should she say?

Unable to bear the tension any longer, she stood up quickly and excused herself, hurrying to their bedroom, her heart sinking as she realised that Nico was close behind her.

He closed the door behind him with an ominous click.

For a long moment he just stared at her, visibly tense, and then he paced across the room to the French windows, clearly at a loss for words.

Finally he stopped dead and faced her, a muscle working in his darkened jaw.

'Again I've misjudged you.'

'It doesn't matter.'

'It *does* matter!' He raked a hand through his dark hair and gave a short laugh. 'I thought that you had chosen me to be her father—'

'Can we just forget it?'

'No. I have been wrong about you so many times. I doubted your love for Rosa but then when she was ill I saw just how deeply you care for her. I assumed that you were hopeless with money but it turned out that you were totally innocent of that crime, too.' His mouth set in a grim line as he ticked off his crimes on his long, strong fingers. 'And if that wasn't enough I then accuse you of conspiring with my sister because you wanted me to father your child. I remember you telling me repeatedly that you weren't lying. I wasn't willing to listen to you then, but I'm listening now.'

'Nico, please…'

Did any of it really matter now? They were married and it was all in the past.

And she loved him.

'I want the truth,' he growled, turning away from her and pacing across their room like a caged tiger. 'And this time I'm listening to every word.'

Abby clasped her hands in front of her and took a deep breath. 'When she found out about Ian, it was Lucia who suggested that I had a baby on my own,' she told him. 'In a way it was my fault that she chose you. I told her that I wanted someone that—'

'Please, don't defend my sister,' he breathed, interrupting her with a lift of his hand. 'I am fast becoming aware that you are every bit as good and kind as you seem. I suspect you wouldn't see bad in anyone.'

'But Lucia—'

'The truth, Abby!'

'She arranged for me to speak to Carlo and then have tests and some counselling. To be honest, I never knew anything about the donor. Then Lucia arranged for me to go to the clinic. I saw a young doctor that I didn't know….' She frowned as she remembered that day, 'I was surprised because I'd been expecting to see Carlo.'

Nico sighed. 'Lucia made sure that you didn't. He knew that I'd agreed to be a donor to a couple in their late thirties.'

Abby didn't know what to say to him. 'I'm sorry.'

'I had never agreed to be a donor for Carlo before,' Nico

continued, 'and she knew it. She knew that if she'd told me the truth, that you were young and single, I never would have agreed.'

'But she meant well.' Abby glanced at him helplessly, daunted by the simmering anger she saw in the depths of his dark eyes. 'She did it because you're her hero. You always were, Nico.'

His mouth twisted into a wry smile. 'You told me that you hadn't chosen me to be the father but I was too arrogant to accept it.'

Abby dipped her head. The whole situation was too embarrassing. 'It isn't your fault,' she mumbled. 'In the circumstances it was a reasonable assumption. Most women think you're the answer to their prayers.'

'But as I am fast discovering, *you* are not most women,' he said dryly, 'and it would have been better for both of us had I realised that a little sooner.'

He was saying that he wished he'd never married her.

She struggled to hide her dismay. 'I don't see that anything has changed,' she said, staring hard at the tiled floor of their bedroom. 'We are still Rosa's parents, and we both still want to be with her.'

'You're staring at the floor again! *Dio*, look at me!' he ordered, exasperation in his deep voice. 'How do you think I feel, knowing that you were frightened of me? Shyness is one thing but the thought that you're scared of me…'

'I'm not scared of you.' Horrified at the mere suggestion, she lifted her head and their eyes met in a clash of fierce awareness.

'But you *were*.'

'Well, it's true that you made me nervous,' she admitted, butterflies coming to life in her stomach as she looked into his incredibly sexy eyes. 'But you were right when you said that it was chemistry. I just didn't recognize it at the time.'

He sucked in a long breath. 'I'm ashamed of the way I

treated you. You were totally innocent and yet I threatened to take your child—'

'Because you thought you couldn't have a family any other way,' Abby said softly, and he rubbed a hand over the back of his neck, his tension pronounced.

'Can you forgive me?'

'What is there to forgive?' She gave a gentle smile. 'Wanting to have your child with you is something to be proud of.'

'But I wanted to punish you.' The honesty of his rough admission made her smile.

'Remind me never to cross you.'

'And remind me always to believe everything you say in the future,' he groaned, dragging her against him and taking control again as always. 'We both love Rosa and that will be enough to make this marriage work.'

Abby swallowed, wishing desperately that he hadn't voiced that last statement.

Although his opinion of her may have altered, his reasons for marrying her hadn't. He'd married her to gain possession of his daughter and nothing was ever going to change that fact.

As the limo moved swiftly through the darkened streets, Abby could hardly believe she was back in London.

And in many ways she didn't want to believe it.

Sardinia had been amazing.

Apart from one afternoon when Nico had gone out with Carlo, they'd spent the entire week in each other's company.

She still felt nervous when he entered the room but it was a different type of nerves. This time she was well aware that it had nothing to do with intimidation and everything to do with sexual awareness.

Awareness of just what he could make her feel in bed.

Not that she had any illusions about Nico. He clearly

enjoyed making love to her because he had spent virtually the whole week doing little else, but she knew that there was no emotion involved.

Such incredible and intimate sex was obviously perfectly normal for him.

'You are very quiet, *cara mia*,' he said suddenly, a frown touching his dark brows as the limo pulled up outside his apartment. 'Are you feeling ill?'

'No.' She gave him a wan smile and reached to undo the straps of Rosa's car seat. 'I—I just enjoyed my time in Italy.'

There was a tense silence and her face heated under his watchful gaze. For a fleeting second she had the impression that he was going to say something else but then Matt opened the door and the moment passed.

Fortunately there was no sign of the press and everything in the apartment was as cool and elegant as ever.

Abby glanced around her, hardly able to believe that only a week had passed since she'd last been here.

Nico was talking into his mobile phone, a frown on his face as he listened to whoever was on the other end.

When he finally flipped it closed his expression was grim. 'I'm sorry to abandon you on our first night back, but I have to go to the hospital.' He raised his hands in a gesture of apology. 'Baby Hubbard has been readmitted and they want me to take a look at her. She might need to have surgery sooner than we'd planned.'

Abby tried to hide her disappointment. 'Will you be back later?'

He was already walking towards the bedroom, preparing to change. 'I hope so, but if not I will see you in the hospital tomorrow and we will have dinner tomorrow night. In the meantime, Matt will be around if you have any problems and Giovanni will cook for you.'

She didn't care about the cooking. She wanted Nico's company.

Which was completely ridiculous, of course. They didn't have that sort of relationship.

No ties. Wasn't that what he'd promised when he'd married her?

They had married for Rosa, not for each other.

She watched as he emerged from the bedroom dressed in a suit that emphasised his height and the width of his shoulders. He was every inch the successful surgeon and she thought regretfully of the way he'd relaxed with her at his home in Sardinia. She'd had a glimpse of part of him that he usually kept hidden from the world. But now the holiday was over and the 'Iceberg' was back.

So what did that mean for their relationship?

'You look fantastic. You obviously had a wonderful week,' Heather said as they watched the night staff leave the ward.

Abby smiled. She *had* had a wonderful week.

In fact, it had been a week like no other.

'And now you're Mrs Santini.' Heather looked at her with awe and Abby shrugged self-consciously.

'I'm still the same person, Heather,' she said awkwardly, but Heather shook her head.

'There are subtle differences. You've got this luminous glow, but I suppose that's just love,' Heather said wistfully.

Abby blushed.

Was it really that obvious?

If it was, she needed to be careful around Nico. The last think she wanted was for him to find out her true feelings for him.

'Well, you're one lucky girl,' Heather said firmly, 'and I don't suppose you're going to be working with us for much longer so I'm making the most of you while I can. I suppose Nico told you that baby Hubbard was readmitted last night?'

Abby nodded and Heather rolled her eyes. 'Well, of course he did. How stupid of me. You live with the man so you ought to know when he's not at home. Anyway, her oxygen saturation has dropped so they're going to operate tomorrow. They're checking that there's a bed in CICU and arranging a theatre slot.'

'And has the mother managed to find anyone to take care of the other children?'

'She has, but she's in a bit of a state.' Heather smiled sheepishly at Abby. 'And that's where you come in, of course. I need you to try and calm her down as she's making the baby stressed. You're always so amazing with the patients.'

'I'll talk to her,' Abby said immediately, and Heather nodded.

'Good. Nico checked her last night for us and he's running a few more tests today, but basically he intends to operate tomorrow. He said he'd be up later to talk to the mother again and get the consent form signed. By the way, baby Hubbard has a name now—Suzy.'

Abby finished updating herself on the changes on the ward and then made her way to the side room to find Suzy and her mother.

Vanessa Hubbard was a thin, stressed-looking woman whose clothes looked slightly too big for her.

The moment Abby walked into the room she looked up with worried eyes.

'Hello, Vanessa, I'm Abby Har— Santini,' Abby corrected herself quickly, shaking the other woman's hand and peeping into the cot at the sleeping baby. 'I'm going to be your nurse. I can imagine just how worried you are so, please, feel that you can ask me anything you want to.'

'Santini?' Vanessa looked startled. 'That's the same name as the surgeon.'

'He's my husband,' Abby said quietly, and Vanessa gave a weak smile.

'You must be very proud of him.'

Abby nodded. She was proud.

Very proud.

'My GP checked him out for me,' Vanessa confessed ruefully, 'and he said that he's one of the best. Not that that is much consolation. I just wish Suzy was OK....'

'Well, of course you do.'

'I thought we were going to have a few weeks at home together but then she started breathing quickly and I couldn't get her to take her bottle.'

'That's because her oxygen saturation dropped,' Abby told her, her eyes flicking to the monitor to reassure herself that the readings were now within normal limits. 'When did she last feed?'

'She had a bottle at six,' Vanessa told her, watching the baby with tears in her eyes. 'I just can't believe this is happening....'

The tears rolled down her cheeks and Abby felt her heart twist for the poor woman.

'It must be awful for you, but try not to upset yourself.' She slipped her arms around the other woman and gave her a hug. 'Isn't there anyone who can be with you?'

Vanessa blew her nose and shook her head. 'No. My parents died a long time ago and Suzy's father left us when I told him I was pregnant again. He said we just couldn't afford another child.'

Tears spilled down her cheeks again and at that moment Nico walked into the room dressed in blue theatre scrubs.

He frowned as he saw that Vanessa was crying. 'Has something happened?'

'She's just very upset and worried about little Suzy,' Abby told him quietly, her arms still round the other woman who was finding it hard to control herself.

'Of course.' His voice was rich and masculine. 'That is understandable. Perhaps it would help if I sat down and went through the operation with you, Vanessa?'

Vanessa sniffed and made a visible effort to pull herself together. 'Thank you. I'd like that. My GP has been great but he said that you were the best person to explain everything.'

Nico glanced at Abby. 'Can we arrange some coffee?'

She nodded, understanding that he wanted to be left alone with Vanessa for a few moments.

By the time she shouldered her way back into the room with two cups of coffee, Vanessa was looking more relaxed. She didn't know what Nico had said, but whatever it was had obviously done the trick.

Abby handed Vanessa a cup of coffee and placed Nico's next to him.

'You understand that the main vessels coming out of your daughter's heart are the wrong way round—we call this transposition of the great arteries. I will show you with a diagram.' Out came the pad and Nico's pen moved smoothly over the paper as he drew the heart. 'This artery takes blood from the heart around the body, this artery takes blood to the lungs, but with Suzy they are in the wrong place.'

Vanessa stared at the diagram and nodded. 'So how is she getting her oxygen?'

'She survived at the beginning because she had what we call a PDA—that stands for patent ductus arteriosus—but you don't need to worry about that bit.' He waved a hand dismissively. 'The PDA connects the two arteries and therefore allows the blood to mix.'

'But she still wasn't getting the oxygen she needed, which was why she was blue?' Vanessa looked at him keenly and Nico nodded, evidently surprised.

'You grasp the problem astonishingly quickly,' he observed, and she blushed at the praise.

'I loved biology at school. I would have loved to have been a doctor but I got pregnant and—' She broke off and gave a shrug. 'Anyway, you don't want to know about that. Carry on.'

'If you remember your biology, you will recall that in a

normal heart blood flows in a series.' He used a fresh piece of paper to demonstrate what he meant and then glanced up at her. 'In TGA there are two separate circulatory patterns.'

'So the two sides don't connect?'

Nico nodded. 'Exactly.'

'So that P— PDA...?' Vanessa glanced at Nico to check she'd got it right '...was the only connection?'

Nico nodded. 'That's right.'

'So how does the operation help?'

'I will basically move the arteries to the correct anatomical position.' Again Nico's pen flew over the page. 'I move this to here, and this to here....'

'And what is the risk of the operation? What are the chances that I might lose her?'

'We quote a risk of five per cent for all our major heart operations,' Nico said quietly, and Vanessa closed her eyes.

'But I don't have a choice, do I? Without the operation she won't survive.'

'That's correct,' Nico's voice was gentle and Vanessa took a deep breath.

'Well, if someone told me I had a five per cent chance of winning the lottery, I'd know that I wouldn't.'

Nico smiled, admiration evident in his dark eyes. 'That is a positive way of looking at it. Today we will need to do a few more tests and get her ready for Theatre tomorrow. The anaesthetist will pop up and see her and Abby will take you for a visit to CICU. It is important to see where she will be taken after the operation or it can be very daunting.'

He answered more of Vanessa's questions and then he examined Suzy.

Finally he moved towards the door. 'We will operate tomorrow. If you have any questions in the meantime, Abby will be able to get hold of me.'

Abby followed him out of the room and he smiled down

at her apologetically. 'I'm sorry about last night. I had intended to come home but things were rather hectic here—'

'It doesn't matter,' she said immediately, trying not to be distracted by the heat in his eyes. 'I was wondering—could I watch you operate on Suzy? I've never seen an arterial switch.'

He nodded immediately. 'Of course. If Heather can spare you, I don't have a problem with that. I will warn the theatre sister. There are quite a few other people watching, too, so you won't be alone.' He checked his watch and pulled a face. 'I have to go. I need to see a patient on CICU.'

Suddenly he seemed miles away from the man she'd spent the last week with. He was driven and focused and thinking about nothing but work. Which was what made him such an exceptional surgeon, of course, she reminded herself. He had incredible self-discipline.

'I'll see you later, then....' Her voice tailed off feebly. She was dying to ask him if he would be coming home, but there was something forbidding about those broad shoulders and the grim set of his mouth. With the gravity of the operations he had to perform, the last thing he needed was her asking him to come home.

He started to walk down the corridor and then turned to face her, a ghost of a smile playing around his mouth.

'By the way, *tesoro*, your coffee is disgusting—remind me to give you lessons.'

Nico didn't come home again that night and Abby lay alone in the enormous bed, a seething mass of frustration.

Before last week she'd never really thought about sex. Her few brief encounters with Ian had been completely unmemorable but since her week with Nico she seemed to have turned into a sex addict.

All she could think about was the way she felt when he made love to her.

Unfortunately he obviously didn't feel the same way, she

thought miserably as she dressed for work next morning and lifted Rosa out of her cot. Since they'd returned home, his entire focus had been his work.

She was under no illusions that he'd married her to get Rosa, but after last week she'd also consoled herself that he enjoyed their love-making.

But maybe she was wrong.

The ward was humming with activity when she arrived and Heather caught her immediately.

'Suzy Hubbard is already prepped for Theatre and ready to go. They rang two minutes ago so if you can grab a porter we can take her down. Her mum is determined to go with her so expect some tears. Once Suzy's under the anaesthetic, you can go into Theatre.'

Abby looked around the bustling ward doubtfully. 'Are you sure that's all right—that we're not too busy?'

Heather shook her head. 'We're fine actually. I've got a brilliant agency nurse on today, which helps, and it's really important for you to see a switch. It's easier to understand the relevance of post-operative care if you've seen what the operation involves.'

Abby phoned for a porter and together they wheeled the cot down the corridor towards the theatre.

Vanessa was pale but in control.

In the anaesthetic room she held the baby in her arms until the anaesthetist had put her under and then she kissed the child gently and left the room with the porter.

One of the theatre nurses stuck her head round the door and looked at Abby. 'Are you watching? Come with me and I'll show you where to scrub.'

Abby followed her instructions to the letter, changing into theatre scrubs and wearing a sterile gown and gloves.

She walked into Theatre, her knees trembling slightly. What would it feel like, seeing Nico operate? She wasn't sure she'd be able to concentrate.

But she was wrong.

She was so mesmerised by the speed and skill of his fingers that all she could think of was what an outstanding surgeon he was.

'This is a standard arterial switch operation,' he told the paediatrician, who was also watching. 'I move the aorta to the left ventricle, and the pulmonary artery to the right ventricle and the coronary arteries to the aorta.'

The paediatrician lifted his eyebrows. 'So basically you're restoring normal anatomy?'

'Precisely. More light, please.'

The theatre nurse adjusted the light and the paediatrician watched, clearly fascinated.

'So how long has this been the operation of choice?'

'In my hospital in Italy, we moved from a Senning to a switch policy some time ago,' Nico told him. 'The Senning procedure was more of a physiological repair—they didn't change the anatomy, but they helped the blood get to the right places. Initially the mortality rate was lower than for the arterial switch.'

'So why did surgeons adopt the switch?'

Nico glanced at the monitors and then at the anaesthetist, assuring himself that everything was all right before he continued. 'It was found that various problems developed 10 to 15 years after the operation. The right and left ventricles have different abilities to cope with pressure and volume work. In patients who've had the Senning operation, the right ventricle has to do the work usually done by the left ventricle and in some patients it was just too much and the heart failed.'

'And what happens then?'

Nico gave a shrug. 'That is a very serious problem. The only real option is to refer the patient for a heart transplant.'

The paediatrician leaned forward to get a closer look at what Nico was doing. 'Could you do a switch operation on them later on?'

'It has been done.' Nico held out his gloved hand and

the nurse immediately gave him the instrument he wanted. 'But it is experimental at this stage.'

'So the switch operation is pretty much used everywhere?'

'Surgical technique has improved in the years since it was first introduced,' Nico murmured, his dark eyes fixed on his tiny patient. 'It's recognised as being the operation of choice for this condition.'

The operation took almost five hours from beginning to end and Abby was starting to get backache and leg-ache when the anaesthetist gave a frown.

'Her pressure is dropping slightly—are you going to be long?'

'I've finished.' Nico glanced at his registrar. 'I'm sending her to CICU with her chest open. It makes it easier to see what is going on and monitor any bleeding,' he told the paediatrician. 'We will close the chest on CICU in twenty-four hours if everything is well. Thank you, everyone.'

He stepped back from the operating table and stripped off his gloves. 'I'm going to shower and check on my patients in CICU then I have a ward round.' He looked at his registrar. 'You have time for a cup of coffee. I'll meet you on the ward in twenty minutes.'

Abby blinked as she watched him stride out of the room, the doors swinging closed behind him.

He was giving his registrar a short break but she was willing to bet that he wasn't taking one himself. His schedule was punishing and yet there was no visible evidence that he was tired.

She made her way up to the ward and Heather immediately asked her to feed a baby who was waiting to go for a cardiac catheterisation.

Abby walked into the kitchen, fetched the correct formula and then returned to the cot to feed the child.

She'd just finished when Nico strolled onto the ward.

He looked impossibly handsome and she felt her heart stumble in her chest.

She wanted him so badly.

It was funny really, she mused. She'd expected marriage to Nico to be torture, but not for this reason. *Not because she'd fallen in love with him.* What an utterly stupid thing to do, she thought helplessly. She was no different from all those other women who'd thrown themselves at him since he'd been a teenager.

As soon as he saw her he walked across the ward and bent down to look at the baby.

'One of Jack's?'

Abby nodded. 'She's going for a catheter tomorrow.'

'Did you find the operation interesting?'

She glanced up shyly, unable to keep the admiration out of her gaze. 'I thought you were amazing,' she said quietly, and he looked amused.

'I wasn't fishing for compliments.'

Of course he wasn't. A man like him didn't have the need for strokes from others. His self-confidence was total.

'It was interesting and I still think you were amazing,' she said simply, and his eyes locked on hers.

Tension simmered between them and Abby felt her body grow warm.

'Will you be home tonight?'

He tensed slightly and his dark eyes narrowed. 'Abby…'

He hadn't slept with her since Sardinia and she was afraid that he was still feeling guilty about what happened with Lucia.

An awful thought struck her.

Maybe he thought that she didn't *want* to sleep with him.

In which case it was up to her to show him that she did.

Taking a deep breath, she returned the baby to the cot and then looked him in the eye, her hands and knees suddenly weak.

She'd never propositioned a man in her life before. What if he rejected her?

'I—I really need to talk to you,' she stammered, glancing over her shoulder to make sure that none of the other staff were nearby.

He frowned slightly. 'Abby, I—'

'Please…' Her voice was urgent and she licked her lower lip in a provocative gesture. Or at least she hoped it was provocative.

Judging from the sudden tension in his shoulders, it had the desired effect.

'I'll try and get home tonight,' he said cautiously, and she shook her head and jerked her head towards the linen cupboard.

If she waited until tonight something would prevent it happening. She'd have lost her nerve or he'd get called back to the hospital.

'Not tonight—*now*! I need to get a clean sheet. Come with me?'

She walked into the tiny linen room and after a few moments he walked in behind her. His eyes never leaving hers, he closed the door firmly behind him, keeping his back to it so that no one else could enter.

'Abby—'

'I want you, Nico,' she breathed huskily, her heart thudding heavily against her chest. If he rejected her she'd die of embarrassment. Trying to forget that they were in a semi-public place, she lifted a hand to the buttons of her uniform and started to undo them one by one.

Nico stood frozen to the spot, visibly stunned by her performance. He seemed incapable of moving, his shocked dark eyes raking over her with blatant incredulity.

She reached the last button and paused, doubt suddenly showing in her huge eyes.

Finally he moved, dragging her against him with a harsh groan, his kiss hard and urgent.

Without lifting his mouth from hers, he slid her uniform up her thighs and gave a groan of satisfaction as he curved his hands over her bottom.

'*Dio mio*, I've missed you so much,' he growled against her mouth. 'If the other doctors knew that you were wearing stockings under this uniform, I'd have to do heart surgery on all of them.'

Swamped by the intense relief that he still wanted her, Abby kissed him back, happy for him to take over the dominant role.

'I really, really can't believe we're doing this *here*,' he said thickly, reaching down and dealing with his zip in a swift movement.

'Well, there didn't seem much choice. You haven't been home for days and I couldn't wait any longer.' Abby was breathing heavily, her body aching with need for him.

'That makes two of us. I want you *so* badly, *cara mia*,' he muttered, turning her swiftly so that she was the one against the door. In a smooth movement he slid his hands up her bare thighs and Abby's breath came in shallow pants as she felt his strong fingers sliding inside her panties and touching her intimately.

'Nico…' She forgot where they were and what the risks were if they were caught. Her brain was swamped by the explosive feelings inside her trembling body.

'You are so wet for me,' he groaned, lifting her so that she straddled him and entering her with a fierce thrust that brought a gasp of ecstasy to her lips.

The feeling was so exquisite, so unbearably exciting that she completely lost control, allowing her body to be totally dominated by his powerful thrusts.

Their mouths locked together as they climaxed violently, both of them stunned into silence by the intensity of what they'd shared.

Nico dropped his forehead to hers and looked deep into

her eyes, his breathing decidedly unsteady. 'That was fantastic, *cara mia.*'

Letting her out of his grasp, he adjusted her uniform so that she was decent.

Abby felt totally shell-shocked.

What was happening to her?

She was a shy, law-abiding person and here she was making wild passionate love in a tiny linen cupboard where they could have been caught at any minute.

Nico zipped his fly in one swift movement and threw her a dizzying smile. 'Now I feel much more relaxed.'

Abby stared at him weakly. She felt as though she'd never walk again.

He touched her cheek gently and suddenly seemed to hesitate. 'There are things I need to tell you—things we need to talk about...' He seemed about to say more but then his bleeper went off and he rolled his eyes. 'But now is clearly not the time. I will *definitely* be home tonight. I will see you there.'

With that he jerked open the door of the linen cupboard and walked out with his usual confidence, not even trying to be discreet.

But it was that very confidence that would probably save them, Abby reassured herself. There was nothing furtive about the way Nico behaved. Looking at him, no one would ever imagine that moments ago he'd been making love.

Which was probably more than could be said for her.

She smoothed her blonde hair, wriggled her hips to adjust her uniform and then made her way back onto the ward, thinking about what Nico had said.

He wanted to talk to her. And it was obviously something serious.

What was he going to say?

CHAPTER NINE

THE phone was ringing when Abby arrived home so after putting Rosa on the floor to play with some toys, she answered the call.

She was still dazed and in shock from her breathlessly exciting encounter with Nico and she fully expected it to be him on the phone.

'Hello?'

But it wasn't Nico, it was Carlo, calling from Italy, and Abby smiled as they exchanged small talk.

'Nico isn't home yet,' she said finally, stooping to remove a shoe from Rosa's mouth. 'Do you want me to give him a message?'

Carlo's voice was warm and friendly. 'No message. I just rang for a chat. I spoke to him last night when I gave him the news, but he was in a rush so we didn't really have time to talk properly. You must be thrilled about it, Abby.'

Thrilled about what?

What news?

'Well—' Abby was about to confess that she'd barely seen Nico since they'd returned from their honeymoon, and the time they *had* spent together had been at the hospital, but Carlo was still talking.

'I told him a year ago to take the test, and that it would probably be all right, but he was too stubborn. All that worry over nothing. At least now he knows that he'll be able to give you as many babies as the two of you can cope with.'

Babies?

Abby froze to the spot. Rosa had the shoe in her mouth

again but this time Abby didn't even bother removing it. She just clutched the phone tighter.

'Abby?' Carlo's voice sounded puzzled. 'Abby, are you there?'

'Yes, I'm here.' Abby plopped down onto the nearest chair, her palms sweaty. 'So—so everything's fine for him, then? He isn't infertile?'

'No way. I did the test for him when you were in Sardinia, but I suppose he told you that.'

No, he hadn't. But that was obviously where he'd been when he'd vanished with Carlo for the afternoon. He hadn't told her anything about what he'd been doing, and why should he? She was nothing but his key to Rosa. He had never wanted to marry her at all. He'd done it to gain custody of his one and only child. But now he could have more children....

Suddenly Abby felt physically sick.

'I have to go, Carlo,' she said quickly. 'I'll get him to call you back.'

She hung up, her fingers shaking, scooped Rosa into her arms and walked in a daze back to the bedroom.

Nico had married her because he'd wanted a family. But now he had discovered that he could have a family of his own. As many children as he liked, with the woman of his choice.

He didn't need to be with her any more.

And that was obviously what he'd been trying to tell her earlier. Which meant that she knew exactly what the conversation would be when he arrived home later.

He already believed that she hadn't wanted to marry him and now he'd discovered that *he* hadn't needed to marry *her* either. Their marriage had been a compromise for both of them, but he no longer needed to make that compromise.

Which meant that the marriage was over.

* * *

An hour later Abby was packed and pacing nervously around the huge living room.

Why on earth hadn't she just left Nico a note?

What was she hoping to achieve by staying to face him?

Was she hoping that he'd beg her to stay?

No, of course not. She knew he wasn't going to beg her to stay, but somehow, even knowing that he didn't love her, she couldn't bring herself to say goodbye on a piece of paper.

Not after everything they'd shared.

She was still wondering whether she should write a note when Nico strolled out of the lift, deep in conversation with someone on his mobile.

Still talking, he tossed his briefcase onto the nearest sofa and then paused, his black eyes narrowing as they homed in on her suitcase.

He ended the conversation abruptly and slipped the phone back into his pocket.

'What are you doing?'

His voice was deceptively calm and Abby felt her heart beat faster.

'I'm making things easy for both of us. I know what you wanted to talk to me about,' she blurted out, wishing that she didn't love him so much. Leaving him was the hardest thing she'd ever had to do in her life. 'I've spoken to Carlo.'

Nico was suddenly still, his lean, handsome face expressionless. 'About what, precisely?'

'I *know*, Nico,' she said softly, trying to hide the pain she felt inside. 'I know that you can have more children. You can have as many children as you like with whoever you like. You don't need me any more.'

Nico said nothing and Abby started to chatter nervously, filling in the gaps herself.

'You can still see Rosa and I'll always talk about you and let her know that she has a father she can be proud of,' she said hoarsely, knowing that if she didn't get away soon she was going to make a total fool of herself, and that was the last thing she wanted. She didn't want to join the ranks of women who'd made fools of themselves over him. She was going to hang onto her dignity if it killed her.

The silence seemed to stretch to infinity. When he finally spoke, his expression gave nothing away. 'So where are you planning to go?'

'I've found a bedsit that's available immediately—'

'A *bedsit*?' Finally he reacted and she couldn't help smiling at his horrified tone. Bedsits obviously rated down there with buses for Nico Santini. His black brows met in an ominous frown. 'Are you seriously telling me that you'd rather live in a *bedsit* than my apartment?'

She swallowed hard. 'I'd rather live anywhere than stay in a loveless marriage. It isn't going to work, Nico. We both know that. In Sardinia you gave me the option to end the marriage. I'm taking that option for both our sakes.'

He looked at her for a long moment and then paced over to the window.

Abby stared at his back helplessly. Wasn't he going to say anything at all about their time together? What was the matter with him?

She'd never known him short of words before.

'We'll be fine,' she muttered finally, stooping to pick up Rosa and her small bag. 'I've taken a few of the clothes. I hope you don't mind, but if you do then obviously I can—'

'I don't care about the clothes,' he grated, tension visible in his powerful shoulders as he turned to face her.

This was agony.

'I really have to go,' she said quickly, picking up Rosa and her bag and giving him a bright smile. 'I'll be in touch so that we can arrange when you want to see Rosa. That's if you want to, of course.'

Without waiting for him to reply, she hurried to the lift

and stepped inside, thumping the button for the foyer and praying for the doors to close quickly.

If she spent any more time in the same room as him, she was going to lose all self-control and throw herself at the man. Walking away from him without confessing just how much she loved him was the hardest thing she'd ever done.

Tears threatened but she refused to let them fall until she was safely away from his building.

She absolutely would not make an exhibition of herself.

As the lift doors opened on the ground floor she hoisted her bag further onto her shoulder and walked across the marbled foyer, stopping as she saw her exit blocked by Matt.

'Wait a moment.' He put one powerful arm across the door and gave her a rueful smile. 'I can't let you go, I'm afraid.'

'It's OK, Matt.' Touched that he was still keeping an eye on her, she gave him a shaky smile. 'Mr Santini knows I'm going.'

But Matt wasn't listening to her. He was staring across at the other lift, relief in his eyes as his boss came striding towards him.

'Just caught her,' he said quietly, and Nico nodded and spoke briefly in Italian.

Without question Matt melted into the background, hovering just out of earshot.

Abby looked at Nico, waiting for him to speak, her heart thundering in her chest so violently that she was amazed he couldn't see it.

'Please, come back upstairs,' he said finally, his dark eyes wary and his shoulders rigid with tension. 'There are things I need to say to you.'

Abby shook her head. She absolutely wasn't capable of a drawn out confrontation.

'I can't, Nico,' she muttered, clutching Rosa more tightly and turning towards the door.

'Abby, wait!' His voice had a rough edge and he caught her arm, preventing her escape. 'Wait—please. Just five minutes, that's all I ask. And then you can go.'

Five more minutes of torture....

She glanced up at him and her attention was caught by the look in his eyes. She'd never seen Nico nervous before, but this time he definitely looked nervous.

Why?

'I've never begged in my life,' he said, a wry smile touching his firm mouth. 'And I would rather that my first experience wasn't in front of my staff.'

Begged?

His staff?

Abby frowned and glanced round the foyer, noticing the doorman and a few other people watching discreetly.

They were his staff?

'I own this building,' he said gently, and she gave a weary smile.

Well, of course he did. That explained why the press had never been near his flat. He was totally protected on the top floor.

'I have had plenty of first experiences since I met you,' he said, his tone slightly bitter, 'but I would prefer that making a spectacle of myself in public wasn't one of them. Would you at least come back up to the apartment with me so that we can talk in private?'

His restrained courtesy was so unlike his usual arrogant, controlling style that her eyes widened.

'You're *asking* me, Nico, not telling me?' She couldn't resist teasing him and he gave a wry smile, the expression on his handsome features a visible admission that he was aware of his own faults.

'As I said, I have had plenty of first experiences with you,' he drawled, 'and asking instead of telling is probably another example.' His smile faded. 'Please, Abby.'

She hesitated and then nodded.

Instantly Nico was back in control, indicating with a snap of his fingers that Matt should take Rosa.

He ushered her into the lift and back into the apartment, not speaking until she was standing in his elegant living room with its amazing view across Hyde Park.

Abby stood there, waiting for the inevitable. He was going to discuss divorce. She knew he was. He'd decided that there was no point in delaying.

'Would you like a drink?'

She shook her head, twisting her hands in front of her and trying to look composed. She hated all this restrained courtesy. She'd actually grown accustomed to his volatile Italian temperament. She liked it. It was part of Nico. Part of who he was.

Nico paced over to the window and then turned to face her, his gaze disturbingly direct. 'I have acted in an unbelievably selfish way since the first day I met you, so I see no reason to change now.' His sensual mouth tightened and he took a deep breath. 'At least hear me out and then if you still want to go I won't stand in your way.'

Abby's heart lurched and her eyes widened. But surely he wanted her to go. She'd expected him to grab the chance to be rid of her with both hands.

'I know what you think of me,' he said roughly, raking a hand through his dark hair, 'and frankly I don't blame you. I've treated you very badly indeed. I bullied you and threatened you and behaved appallingly. I never once listened to your side of a story or considered your situation. I forced you into a marriage that you must have found totally abhorrent and yet you haven't complained. All you have done is shown unstinting love for our daughter and kindness to my family, especially my sister who is extremely fortunate to have such a loyal and forgiving friend.'

Stunned by his admission of guilt, Abby stared at the floor, thoroughly embarrassed by his gruffly spoken words. He made her sound like some sort of saint.

'Nico, I—'

'If you're about to say that none of it matters, please, don't,' he ground out, pacing across the carpet with such restrained violence that she blinked in surprise. 'I'm only too aware that I've been a lousy husband to you.'

Lousy husband?

She opened her mouth to deny it but he was still in full flow.

'My only defence is that I wasn't thinking rationally. When I had the cancer diagnosis I was devastated.' He paced over to the window, staring out across the park. 'Like most people, I had always believed myself to be immortal. It came as a shock to realise that I wasn't. Until then I'd always believed that I was totally in control of my life.'

She walked over to him and put a hand on his arm, her touch gentle. 'It must have been terrible for you.'

He shrugged dismissively. 'They did what they needed to do and I was lucky. The disease hadn't spread and they are confident that there will be no recurrence. But I was told at the time that it was very likely that I would be infertile. I was given the opportunity to freeze sperm before my treatment but I just wanted the disease treated as soon as possible.'

'But you never actually had a test until Carlo did one last week?'

He gave a short laugh and shook his head. 'No.'

'You just assumed you'd never be able to have children.'

'Which was why I decided to find out how the one baby I had fathered was doing.' His jaw tightened and he didn't look at her. 'That was when I discovered the deception.'

'It must have been very painful for you to see your child with a young single mother,' she said quietly. 'I can totally understand your frustration. You had so much to offer a child and yet were unable to have one of your own.'

He turned to look at her, his expression incredulous. 'How can you be so generous? I stormed into your house that night and threatened to take your daughter away from you.'

'But you believed that I'd lied to you,' she said, easily able to understand how he must have felt in the circumstances and willing to defend him. 'You believed that she would have been better off with you.'

'I was arrogant and unforgivably rude.' He sighed and rubbed a hand over the back of his neck in a visible effort to relieve the tension. 'I pretended that I was concerned for Rosa's welfare but the truth was I was just being selfish. I thought that she represented my only chance to be a father and I was determined to take that chance, no matter what. I searched around for reasons to justify taking her and I'm ashamed for having intimidated you. I remember how hard it was for you to look me in the eye that night. It was a testament to just how much you loved Rosa that you stood up to me.'

Her eyes teased him gently, her hand still on his arm. 'Apologising, Nico?'

He gave a wry smile. 'Yet another first.' He turned slightly and covered her hand in his. 'You are the only woman I have ever met who showed absolutely no interest in me or my money, and you were the first woman to say no to me.'

Abby couldn't resist smiling. 'Not that you listened.'

'That's because I haven't heard it that often in my life,' he confessed ruefully. 'I was so stunned when you told me that I was the last man on earth you'd want to marry that I didn't even believe that you meant it.'

Abby's smile faltered. Had she really said that? She must have been totally deluded.

'And this brings me to the hardest part of all.' He cupped her face in his hands and forced her to look at him. 'I know you didn't want to marry me, but I want you to stay. Please.'

She stared at him, unable to believe what she was hearing.

'You want me to still be your wife?' She must have sounded as incredulous as she felt because his hands dropped from her face and his dark eyes were shuttered.

'It is too much to contemplate, clearly.' He moved away from her but she moved after him, hardly daring to ask the question that needed to be asked.

'Why do you want me to stay, Nico?'

He turned slowly, his eyes wary. 'Why do you think?'

'I don't know.' Suddenly she was aware of every beat of her heart. 'I assumed that you didn't, which was why I was leaving.'

His eyes were suddenly sharp. 'You were leaving because you thought I wanted you to?'

She nodded. 'That's right. Now that you can have babies, you can have them with any woman you choose.'

His gaze burned into hers. 'And what if I choose you?'

There was an electrified silence. 'Me…?'

'Yes, you.'

'But you married me because you wanted Rosa….' Her voice faltered and he moved towards her and took her hands in his.

'That's true. But I want to *stay* married to you because I love you,' he said quietly. 'I have never said those words to another human being in my life. I didn't believe love existed, but I was wrong about that, too.'

He loved her?

Dazed with shock, Abby stared at him. 'How—? I didn't know—'

'I didn't know myself until I saw the lift doors close,' he confessed, stroking a long finger down her flushed cheek. 'Then I suddenly realised that if I let you walk out of my life I would have lost everything that mattered to me.'

He loved her.

Abby stared at him. 'You're asking me to stay?'

He frowned. 'Not exactly asking. I'm not great at asking, as you know by now.' His dark eyes gleamed with wry amusement. 'I'm actually *telling* you to stay. I've had enough firsts for one day. From now on I'm back to my autocratic, controlling self.'

She felt light-headed with happiness. 'And what if I don't want to?'

'You do want to, Abby.' He was arrogantly sure of himself and the expression in his eyes was so sexy that she felt the heat curl deep in her stomach. 'I know you love me....'

Her eyes widened in consternation. 'How do you know?'

'Dragging me off for rampant sex in the linen cupboard was a slight clue,' he drawled, amusement in his dark eyes as she blushed scarlet.

She gave a groan of embarrassment and buried her face in his broad chest. 'Don't remind me.'

'On the contrary, I intend to remind you frequently, *tesoro*,' he teased gently. 'If I needed any more evidence that you loved me, that was it. You are naturally reserved and I am well aware that displaying your desire for me in a public place said a great deal about the way you feel about me.'

She wasn't willing to let him have the upper hand just yet. 'Maybe I don't love you. Maybe I just enjoy good sex....' She smiled.

'*Sì*, that is undoubtedly true, thank goodness.' He hauled her hard against him so that she felt the heat of his arousal pressing through the fabric of her dress. 'But the reason it was so good was the strong love we both feel for each other.'

He lowered his head and took her mouth in a drugging kiss that left them both dazed.

Eventually she lifted her eyes to his. 'So you're really asking me to stay married to you?'

He shook his head and claimed another kiss. 'Not asking. Telling.'

Her eyes teased him. 'And if I agree to stay married, you promise you won't intimidate me?'

'I'll try not to.' He kissed his way down her neck and she gasped.

'And when I say no, will you listen?'

He paused and then lifted his head, his expression wicked. 'That depends on when you say it.' He flashed her a smile that made her insides tumble over. 'If we are making love then I'm afraid I can't promise to listen.'

Despite the teasing note in his voice, she knew there was an element of truth in what he said. There probably would be occasions when he'd be controlling and overbearing, but she also knew that it was just one of the many things that she loved about him.

'I'm not saying no at the moment,' she said huskily, and his dark eyes gleamed and he swept her up in his arms and walked towards the bedroom.

'I love you.' He laid her gently on the bed and came down on top of her, all dominant, virile male.

'And I love you.' Her breathing rapid, she reached up and touched his face. 'So what am I going to do about my bedsit?'

He laughed and rolled onto his back, hauling her with him. 'Is this a good time to confess that I don't actually know what a bedsit is?'

Pressed against his powerful body, Abby was having trouble concentrating. 'You don't?' She broke off as he slid her skirt up her thighs and positioned her to take him. 'Nico!'

This time the excitement of his love-making was almost unbearable and when she finally collapsed against him she felt tears on her cheeks.

'Don't cry, *tesoro*.' He brushed them away with a gentle finger. 'No more tears, ever. My sole purpose in life is to make you and Rosa happy and keep you both safe. And you have to promise no more bedsits—whatever they are—and no more buses. From now on you are mine.'

He said it with such a smug note of possession in his voice that she should have objected, but how could she when she wanted nothing more than to be his?

'Agreed.' She looked him in the eye and dropped a kiss on his mouth. 'But will you do something for me?'

He smiled at her indulgently. 'Anything.'

'I want you to forgive Lucia and make your peace.'

He groaned and closed his eyes briefly. 'That girl is a minx.'

'If it weren't for her, we wouldn't be together,' Abby pointed out softly, and his eyes flew open, passion burning in the dark depths.

'Don't even remind me of that,' he growled, holding her so tightly that she could barely breathe. 'All right, I'll call her later tonight.'

'She did us a favour, Nico,' Abby reminded him as she snuggled against his powerful frame, and she felt him laugh.

'Well, for goodness' sake, don't tell her that or she'll be matchmaking for Carlo next.'

Abby lifted her head, suddenly interested. 'I love your brother.' She saw the ominous look in his dark eyes and bent to kiss him. 'Not in the way that I love you—but he's such a nice person. I can't believe he doesn't have a woman….'

'He has plenty of women,' Nico drawled, trailing a hand gently up her spine. 'But when you're wealthy it becomes very hard to trust people. What he needs is a woman like you who would choose a—a *bedsit* instead of life with a man who she believed didn't love her.'

'I'll tell you a secret.' Abby smiled. 'I would have *hated* it.'

'Good,' Nico said arrogantly, rolling her until she was underneath him. 'From now on the only place you're going to live is with me.'

'And that suits me just fine, Signor Santini,' she whispered, her heart thumping as he lowered his head again. 'That suits me just fine.'